"Help!"

She screamed just before her attacker's left hand pressed against her throat, cutting her off, her voice now gurgling like water circling a drain.

Terror threatened to overwhelm her. There was no chance at all that her cries had been heard. Not with the noise from the block party. She could only pray Polly was safely tucked out of sight, curled up in one of her better hiding places, away from the assailant.

She raised her foot and jabbed it backward, then took off in a sprint, bounding toward the front door.

Faster, faster.

The man was only a few steps behind her.

If only she could make it outside, she could ask someone to call 911.

But she needed to stay alive long enough to do that. The man was close and getting closer. She wasn't going to make it.

Think, think.

The powder room was only a few steps away! Once inside the room, she turned the latch and engaged the lock. She needed to make every second count.

Jaycee Bullard was born and raised in the great state of Minnesota, the fourth child in a family of five. Growing up, she loved to read, especially books by Astrid Lindgren and Georgette Heyer. In the ten years since graduating with a degree in classical languages, she has worked as a paralegal and an office manager, before finally finding her true calling as a preschool Montessori teacher and as a writer of romantic suspense.

Books by Jaycee Bullard

Love Inspired Suspense

Visit the Author Profile page at LoveInspired.com.

PROTECTING THE LITTLEST WITNESS

JAYCEE BULLARD

LOVE INSPIRED SUSPENSE
INSPIRATIONAL ROMANCE

LOVE INSPIRED® SUSPENSE
INSPIRATIONAL ROMANCE

Recycling programs
for this product may
not exist in your area.

ISBN-13: 978-1-335-59940-7

Protecting the Littlest Witness

Love Inspired
22 Adelaide St. West, 41st Floor
Toronto, Ontario M5H 4E3, Canada
www.LoveInspired.com

Printed in U.S.A.

When I consider thy heavens, the work of thy fingers,
the moon and the stars, which thou hast ordained;
What is man, that thou art mindful of him?
and the son of man, that thou visitest him?
—*Psalms* 8:3-4

To my mom
And with great thanks to my editor, Katie Gowrie,
for her support and kindness.

ONE

Etta Mitchell had learned about the block party from one of the neighbors. The details had followed two days later in an invitation shoved under her door.

> Come early. Leave late. And bring a smile and a hot dish to share.

Not to be rude, but it didn't sound like her kind of scene. She'd tossed the flyer in the trash and hadn't given it another thought until, days later, a steady buzz of music and laughter leaking through the windows reminded her of the event.

"We'll make our own party," Etta said to the little girl perched next to her on a stool. "What do you think, Polly? Pancakes for dinner sound okay?"

She wasn't surprised when her niece didn't

answer. Polly wasn't talking much these days. Actually, she wasn't talking at all.

Etta tried again with a singsong rhyme set to an old tune she remembered from pre-school.

"Patty cake, patty cake, baker's man. Bake me a cake as fast as you can. Count the eggs out, one, two, three. Just enough to make pan-cakes for my sweetheart and me."

A ghost of a grin lit up Polly's face, causing Etta's heart to leap in her chest. Maybe this was the day she'd break through the wall of silence hampering her attempts to communicate with her niece. But as Etta gripped the cast-iron skillet hanging over the stove, the pan slipped from her hand and clattered against the countertop, causing Polly to dash from the room.

A wave of exasperation pulled at Etta. She closed her eyes and tried to picture her sister's face. *Oh, Lilly. I'm making a mess of this. I'm trying my best, but Polly misses you so much. And every time I start making headway, she runs away.*

The creaking of hinges sent Etta's senses on high alert. It didn't take much to set her heart racing these days, not after what had happened to her sister. But it seemed unlikely that Polly had gone outside just now. Her niece knew the rules, having been told more times than Etta could count that she should never leave the house without permission. But maybe she had forgotten. After all, she was only five.

"Polly...?"

There was a movement to the left, followed by the thudding of heavy footsteps by the patio door. Not Polly, then. Panic threaded through Etta's veins as her eyes darted toward her phone lying on the desk. But as she moved to grab it, stubby fingers cuffed her wrists and a calloused hand clamped across her lips.

"Relax, and no one gets hurt," the man said gruffly.

Etta didn't believe that. Her survivor instinct took over, and she opened her mouth and bit down hard.

"Oww!" the burly intruder howled as he released his hold.

"Help!" she screamed as her attacker's left hand pressed against her throat. "Help," she cried out again, her voice gurgling like water circling a drain.

Terror threatened to overwhelm her. And fear—not just for herself, but for Polly—

gnawed at her senses. She could only hope and pray that the little girl was curled up in one of her favorite hiding places, safe from the assailant. She raised her foot and bent it backward, kicking the man in the groin, and then took off toward the front door.

She rounded the corner into the hall. But her pursuer was close and getting closer, muttering threats as he closed the gap between them, gaining ground with each thunderous step.

"You can run, but I'm gonna catch you."

Her brain registered the details of his heavy footfalls and booming voice even as she realized she'd never make it out the door.

She ducked into the powder room, quickly turning the lock as her pursuer's fists began to hammer against the door. She tamped down her panic and focused on her next move. The only path of escape was through the window above the toilet, seemingly too high to reach and too narrow to shimmy through. But she had to try.

Climbing onto the tank and stretching on tiptoes, she strained her fingers toward the ledge. She could almost touch it. Almost. But not quite. It remained mere inches away.

Bending her legs, she sprang upward,

stretching her arms out, and this time she was able to grab hold of the windowsill. She dangled for a moment to catch her breath and then pulled herself up on her elbows. With the cuff of her sweatshirt tugged across her left hand, she slammed her fist against the sealed window. A cobweb of cracks formed on the glass.

She punched back again. A red stain of blood soaked through the cloth as she brushed aside the jagged glass in the frame. A gust of wind blew through the opening, stinging her face with an exhilarating slap of fresh air.

She swung her right leg upward so that she was straddling the ledge. The crack of the bathroom door crashing off its hinges fueled her desperation. She took a deep breath and readied for the dismount.

But before she could make her move, a cold hand grabbed hold of her ankle, and fingers clenched around her calf. She screamed for help even as her captor held her tight, and she slowly slid down and away from the window. The hand reached up now and encircled her waist, heaving her backward and tossing her to the floor. Pain exploded through her body as she looked up into the sullen eyes of her attacker.

* * *

Steven Hunt walked slowly down the flagstone path that led to the house at 411 Dogwood Drive. The Google map on his phone claimed that this was the right address, but now that he was here, he was second-guessing his decision for the impromptu visit. As for the bouquet of yellow roses he'd purchased on impulse at the bus station, he didn't feel so great about those, either. The flowers had seemed like such a good idea when he'd hopped the bus from Dallas to Silver Creek. Now, not so much.

He wasn't ready for this. Maybe he should just turn around and take his roses along with him. A deep breath brought a sharp jab of pain that ricocheted across his chest and reminded him of what it felt like to be trampled by a two-thousand-pound bull. The doctor had said that it would take a few months for his ribs to heal, but patience had never been his strong suit. He glanced at the front door again, resolution firming in his gut. Wouldn't he regret it even more if, after traveling all this way, he didn't even make the effort to see Etta? Besides, what else was he going to do? Return to South Dakota and his family's smothering sympathy? No, he was here now, and he wasn't ready to go home. He took a step forward, and then froze at the high-pitched and desperate sound of a woman screaming.

Was that Etta?

It was hard to tell amid the cacophony around him—he seemed to have stumbled upon a block party. There was music playing, and people milling about. Another scream came from within the house. He dropped the flowers, sprinted up the steps and pulled at the handle of the front door.

Locked. Following the voices down the hall, he dashed toward the back of the house and raced across the patio and through the half-open glass door, stopping short at the sight of Etta's body sprawled on the kitchen floor.

A huge man hovered beside her, and he didn't look pleased to see someone new preparing to enter the fray.

Steven propelled himself forward, managing to knock the behemoth off balance by the sheer force of the attack.

But Steven's success was short-lived as, a second later, he found himself summarily tossed onto the floor. Fresh pain exploded through Steven's chest as he skidded into a shelf. Books rained down on his back, adding insult to injury. He pushed himself up off the ground and staggered toward the larger man, his arms raised and his fists ready. It had been a while since he'd been in a real brawl, but growing up with a twin brother, he'd been in his share of fights.

He swung his right arm in a hook, his fist connecting with his opponent's chin. He followed with an upward thrust from his left side into the gut. Once again, the element of surprise gave him an initial advantage as the big man staggered backward. But he managed to steady himself and pop a punch at Steven. With a quick step to the right, Steven dodged the blow, but a second one landed squarely against his jaw. The impact made his eyes water and brought a new throbbing ache. He couldn't afford another direct hit. Not in the condition he was in. If his opponent landed a punch to his chest, it would be game over. But how long could he dodge the blows from the man lunging after him?

All of a sudden, Etta appeared behind his attacker, a cast-iron skillet in her hand. She raised her arm and brought down the heavy pan on the man's head. His assailant froze for a moment before his body crumpled to the floor, a thin pool of blood forming around his jaw.

A gasp formed in Steven's throat. Grim-faced with tension, Etta lifted the frying pan a second time and held it above her head. "Don't move," she said, pointing at him. "Who are you and why are you here?"

Not quite the reception he'd been hoping for. "I know it's been fifteen years," Steven began, "but I was expecting at least a glimmer of recognition."

Etta glared back at him for a moment before a look of bewilderment played across her features. "Steven?"

"Got it in one."

The hardness was gone from her voice, but a wary edge remained. "What are you doing here?" she asked, lowering the pan.

"Fair question. But maybe we'd better deal with the matter at hand. What did I just walk into? What's going on?"

"In a minute, okay?" Etta blinked a few times as her gaze took in the body of the man lying face up on the floor. She had hit him hard, and he wasn't moving. Her face seemed to crumple as shock set in.

She kneeled beside her assailant and checked his vitals. From the frown creasing her lips,

Steven assumed that there was no pulse and no sign of breathing. Etta waited a few seconds and then placed the palm of her hand in the middle of the fallen man's chest. Placing her other hand on top of the first, she pushed down hard to perform several dozen compressions.

"Etta…" Steven said.

She looked up at him and shook her head.

He watched as she tilted the man's head and checked his airway, pinched his nose shut and, with her mouth against his, executed two quick rescue breaths. When his chest failed to rise, she repeated the procedure a second time and then a third. She seemed to be preparing for a fourth round of compressions when he realized that he needed to intervene.

He took a step toward her and touched her shoulder.

"Etta, he's gone."

"Pease, God. No," she whispered, dropping her face to her hands.

Steven took a step closer and pulled her toward him. He could feel the drum of her heartbeat as she gulped in a fresh lungful of air.

"I'll call nine-one-one. And when the police get here, I'll explain…"

"No!" Etta pulled away from his embrace and shook her head.

"Etta…you killed the guy. In self-defense, but it needs to be reported."

She glanced down at her fallen attacker and then raised her gaze to meet Steven's. "I can't do that."

Frustration bit at the corners of his mind. How had he forgotten about Etta's stubbornness? He tugged at his beard. "Why not? What's going on? What is it that you aren't telling me?"

"What am I not telling you?" Etta's voice was tinged with hysteria. "What are *you* not telling me? What are you even doing here? You show up at my sister's house fifteen years too late and ask what I'm not telling you."

Fifteen years too late? What did that mean? But now was not the time for that sort of question. He needed to convince Etta to be sensible, to think of the consequences before she committed to a reckless course of action.

"I saw on the news that Lilly died, and I wanted to reach out and tell you that I—"

"No," she said shaking her head. "Lilly didn't just die. She was murdered." She looked as if she was trying to keep her face from crumpling on those words.

"I know that. And I'm sorry for your loss." But the way Etta was acting didn't make any sense. A man was lying dead in the middle of the kitchen floor. They had to call 911 and report the accident to the police. "Are you worried that the break-in today is connected to what happened to your sister?"

"I don't know. I don't know anything for sure. Except that I won't involve the police. If I do, I'll end up arrested, just like Greg."

"Wait. Who's Greg?"

"Lilly's husband. The police think they have him dead to rights for the murder. But they're wrong." She pinned him with her gaze. "Greg would never hurt Lilly. He loved her more than life itself."

Okay, this was getting complicated. Steven raked his chin with his hand and tried to figure out what to do next. "Let's see what we can find out about this guy who attacked you. Then, we really need to talk about reporting the incident. Okay?"

He didn't wait for an answer as he leaned over and patted the man's pockets, pulling out a billfold and reading aloud the information on the license. "Reginald Taylor, age thirty-two, with a home address in Dallas. Ring any bells?"

She shook her head.

He continued his search. A fifty-dollar bill

was tucked under one of the side flaps of the wallet, and as he pushed it back into position, a photograph fluttered to the ground.

"Any idea of who this is?" he asked, holding up a picture of a little girl.

All the color seemed to drain out of Etta's face. "That's Polly," she said.

"Polly?"

"My niece. Lilly and Greg's daughter."

A thread of foreboding snaked its way down his spine. "And where is Polly now?"

"Probably hiding in her room. Just like she did when Lilly was murdered. I should see if I can—"

Ding dong.

Steven's eyes met Etta's as the chime of the doorbell echoed through the house.

"What now?"

TWO

Etta peered through the peephole on the front door. "It's my neighbor, Lynn Weber," she whispered. "She's kind of a busybody."

Bad timing for them. "Will she go away if you don't answer?"

"Maybe. But she'll probably come back to make sure everything is okay."

"Better see what she wants then."

Etta clicked the lock and cracked the door, pressing her body tightly against the opening.

"Hi, Lynn. How are you? Sounds like the block party is going strong."

"Everyone seems to be having a blast. I'm just sorry that you can't join us," the woman replied. "But I totally understand. After all, you're still dealing with the pain of losing your sister. The last thing you need is all that noise and commotion. But I wanted to bring over some cookies for Polly before they all disappeared. Oatmeal-raisin. She's not allergic or anything, is she?"

"Not at all," Etta said, taking the foil-wrapped plate from her neighbor's hand and setting it on the table next to the door, giving Steven a quick view of an older woman with neatly coiffed hair waiting on the threshold. "I'll find Polly and tell her you brought her a treat. Thanks for thinking of us, Lynn. Maybe I'll see you sometime later in the week."

Etta didn't wait for a reply as she pushed the door closed and then turned to face Steven. "We need to find Polly and get out of here now."

Get out of here now? Why was Etta so insistent about cutting the police out of the equation? Wouldn't fleeing the scene make her appear guilty? It wasn't like she had intentionally murdered the guy.

"But, Etta…"

"You need to trust me on this, Steven." Etta's tone was tinged with impatience. "Greg's in jail, and Lilly's gone. That leaves me. I'm the only one left to take care of Polly. It's a mess, and I understand if you don't want to get involved. With this or with us. I can handle it alone."

Steven pulled in a long sigh. "Well, at the

very least, let me help you find Polly. If you called out and said you needed her, would she come?"

"No. And she's really good at hunkering down and keeping quiet. It's sort of her specialty. She hasn't spoken a word since Lilly died."

Steven suddenly felt overwhelmed by a situation that was becoming more confusing by the minute. "Is there a chance that she wandered out into the yard?"

"Maybe."

Steven glanced out the kitchen window. A chain-link fence enclosed a wide lawn with a large wooden play structure. No trees. Just a few scraggly bushes next to a raised flower bed. Unless the kid had dug a tunnel, there weren't that many options for her to hide out there.

"How about you check outside while I search upstairs? It might rouse suspicions if someone sees me wandering around the property."

"Okay. But Polly can be really high-strung. Especially around strangers."

"Don't worry. If I find her, I'll tell her that I'm a friend of her aunt's. I can even show her a picture to prove it." He pulled out his wallet and unfolded a photograph of him and Etta at the lake. Though he had been carrying that particular photo around for years, he couldn't recall the last time he'd looked at it. Wow, did they look young. And happy.

The staircase leading to the upper landing was lined with photographs. Lilly's blue eyes and curly hair—so different from Etta's—made her instantly recognizable as the surly teen he'd met long ago. The man standing next to her, with an arm swung across her shoulders, had to be her husband, Greg. And, of course, there were plenty of pictures of Polly.

At the top of the stairs, Steven paused and listened. It was a tactic he had learned playing hide-and-seek with his twin brother. If you stood completely still and waited, the person you were looking for would invariably make a sound.

But his tactic didn't seem to be working with Polly.

Four doors opened out to the upstairs hall—two bedrooms, a bathroom and what looked to be an office. He checked the bathroom first, flipping the lid on a hamper and scanning behind the towels on the narrow bathroom shelves, but had no success.

He moved toward the office, with its large window that overlooked the backyard. Glancing out, he could see Etta make her way to the top of the play structure to check under the green canopy roof. Even from a distance, he could see her shoulders tense as she bent to scrutinize the top of the slide. He scanned the rest of the office for likely hiding places. There was no closet, but he checked under the desk and even inside a filing cabinet.

There was no sign of Polly.

Two down and two to go. He headed down the hall and into what was clearly the little girl's bedroom. Piles of stuffed animals, most of them horses of every shape and size, covered a large swath of the braided rug that encircled the floor. After pushing aside a handmade quilt, he bent and looked under the bed and then moved on to the closet, determined not to let even the smallest space go unchecked.

Next door was the larger bedroom belonging to Lilly and Greg. Muted gray curtains and crisp white sheets showcased a well-coordinated decorating effort. On the top of a pale wood dresser, Etta's suitcase was open, her clothing still neatly folded with a leather-bound Bible on top of her things. Well, that was new. The Etta he used to know never had a whole lot of time for the Lord. Not that she had ever been hostile to his own faith, just coolly ambivalent.

He once again checked under the bed and in the closet with no success. Where could the little girl be?

The pit in Etta's stomach felt emptier with each passing second as the reality of what had happened seeped into her brain.

She had killed a man. She, Etta Mitchell. A nurse. Someone whose job was to save lives. Instead, she had ended a life in a moment of need and panic and fear.

A case could be made that her that actions had been justified, that if she hadn't grabbed that frying pan, the intruder probably would've killed both her and Steven. And Polly, too, once he found her. After all, her niece seemed to be his target. Fear crept along her spine—she'd felt sick seeing that photo of Polly pulled from the man's pocket. Why would anyone be after her niece? Unless…she and Greg were right that the little girl might have seen something the day Lilly was murdered. What Steven said about her actions being in self-defense was true, though it didn't make dealing with the reality of what she'd done any easier. But there was no way around it. The only thing that mattered was protecting Polly. But with all her hiding and not talking and the nightmares and the fear, that was proving to be difficult.

She clenched her fingers in frustration. She had checked every nook and cranny in the yard that was big enough to fit a five-year-old child. And given the fact that she hadn't heard from Steven, she could assume that he hadn't found Polly, either.

She was getting ready to head back into the house when her gaze settled on a gray plastic storage unit nestled flush against the sidewall. How had she missed it? The container wasn't huge, but it was certainly big enough to accommodate a little girl. Beads of perspiration formed on her forehead as she hurried across the lawn, her knees buckling beneath her as she tore open the lid. But the only thing inside was a coiled-up hose, cracked and forgotten—yet another sign of her failure as keeper of the home. Since Greg had been arrested, not once had she even thought about watering the bushes along the fence. No wonder their leaves were brittle and anemic. A young neighbor kid stopped by weekly to mow the grass, though at this point it was brown and dry as well.

Why hadn't Greg given her better instructions about her duties before he was hauled off to jail? He probably assumed she understood the basics—buy groceries, water the plants, check the mail. And he did have more important things to think about, like mounting an effective defense against the charges being brought by the DA.

From the beginning, Etta had believed there was no way that Greg could have been involved in her sister's murder. He'd always been the rock in their relationship, steady and patient as a foil to her sister's more tempestuous temperament. But lately, she had started to wonder. The police seemed convinced that he alone had both motive and opportunity. What if it turned out they were right? Then, Polly would be left without a mother and a father, forced to live with a hapless aunt who couldn't even remember to water the lawn. And that was best-case scenario. What if Etta herself was arrested for killing an unarmed man? What would happen then?

Etta knew the answer without even pausing to think. Polly would be taken to Child Protective Services, where she would be assigned to a caseworker and become a part of the system. She had seen it all before, first-hand, with Lilly. Sure. There were great foster homes with kind people who loved kids. But her own experience was hardly a recommendation for that type of care.

Tears formed in the corners of her eyes, but she quickly brushed them away. It wouldn't do to have Steven see her crying. No doubt, he was already confused by the current situation. Why had he come to Silver Creek, anyway, especially today, of all days? She supposed she should be grateful to him for saving her life. But seeing him brought back too many painful memories, and she couldn't cope with any of that today.

And how odd that he still had that old photograph of the two of them, taken at the lake. Her own copy had been tossed in the trash immediately after he'd left town in an angry huff, furious that she'd broken their engagement just one day after he had proposed. Why would she keep it? What was the point of holding on to such a tangible sign of love so quickly lost?

There was no point. And the last thing she needed to do today was to get tangled up in regrets about the past. Right now, she needed to find Polly.

An idea she had dismissed just a short time ago as unlikely suddenly seemed reasonable and…likely. Polly knew about the block party and the pony rides for kids eight and under at the end of the block. And the chance for even a few minutes in the saddle would be like catnip to a horse-crazy little girl.

Etta slipped out the gate and headed toward a group that had congregated in her neighbor's front yard. A tall bespectacled man, whom she recognized as the owner of the duplex two doors down, welcomed her with a wide smile.

"Hi. Etta, right? I'm Griffin Galvin. We met at the funeral, though I don't suppose you remember. I'm so sorry for your loss." His smile faded briefly. "Lilly and Greg were good people, and I know I speak for all the neighbors in offering to help in any way possible. Why don't you grab something to eat and come on over and join us at our table?"

Etta barely had time to make her excuses when a young woman approached her, her forehead pleated with concern.

"I was hoping to see you today, Etta. Not sure you remember, but I'm Jenny Sandquist. I was a friend of Lilly's." There was a slight pause before she added, "And your brother-in-law, too. How is he doing? When's the trial? Sorry. I just launched right in without even asking about you. How are you getting along?"

The neighbors' compassion touched her, though she was in a rush. "I'm doing okay."

"I'm glad to hear it," Jenny said. "My kids have been begging for a playdate with Polly. We're totally open to any day next week. Whatever works with your schedule."

"Can I get back to you on that? I'm actually looking for Polly right now. Have you seen her anywhere on the block?"

The woman's blond ponytail swung back and forth as she shook her head. "No-o-o. But I've been a bit distracted snapping pictures of the party to post on the neighborhood-share app. Come to think of it, your niece might be in one of the photos. Let's see if we can spot her." She opened the camera on her phone. "Oh, look at this one. John Pearnin with his chef's hat and apron cooking burgers for the crew. Cute. Oh, and here's one from this morning, before the party got started. That's my older daughter, Ellie, holding baby Mae…"

A series of loud bangs and crackles split the air, sending Etta's heart lurching in her chest. Fireworks exploded at the end of the block.

"Those dads are all just kids at heart! Oh, and take a look at this one," Jenny said, once again holding up her phone. "It's from last summer. Kids from the neighborhood in Lynn's pool."

Etta pulled in a deep breath. She didn't have the time or patience to watch as Jenny scrolled through every single picture on her phone, especially since Polly might still be out here, somewhere, in the middle of the crowd.

"Thanks. Maybe I could look at your pictures later," she said. Suddenly, the idea of milling through the crowds of neighbors at the block party didn't seem like a good idea. But before she could return to the safety of the house, a tall man with a full gray beard stepped in front of her, barring the way.

"You seem upset," he said, positioning himself directly in front of Etta. "Sorry to be so blunt, but I pride myself on reading people's moods. I can always sense if something is wrong."

Etta stared at the man, confused. He was acting as if they were acquainted, but she didn't remember meeting him at the funeral. Maybe she had forgotten. She had forgotten quite a bit about that day.

"Thank you for your concern, but I'm

fine. I was just, um, looking for my niece. I thought she might have wandered off to see the ponies."

The man stepped closer. "I'm headed there right now. Why don't you come with me, and I can help you look for the kid."

Etta took a short step backward and eyed the stranger. Maybe he was exactly who he claimed to be, a neighbor that wanted to help. But she couldn't take that chance. She glanced around, desperate for an excuse to escape.

"Excuse me, I just remembered that I need to talk to Jenny," she said. "But thanks for your offer to help. Maybe I'll talk to you later."

She turned and began to jog toward the adults gathered by the dessert table, but swerved at the last minute and headed toward the gate. Was the bearded man following her? She didn't stop to check.

It was only after she reached the safety of her yard that she was finally able to breathe. But fear still threatened to overwhelm her senses. Her stomach roiled, and her throat tightened. Suddenly, she was running as fast as her feet could carry her. She stumbled into the house, careening into Steven as she turned the corner into the hall.

"There's a man out there, Steven." Her

breath came out in sudden bursts. "He has a long gray beard, and there's something about him that just doesn't seem right. We need to find Polly and escape." She bent over, her hands splayed out across her knees as she struggled for breath.

"I found her, Etta. Don't worry. She's okay," Steven said.

"What? Where?" Even as relief flooded her veins, she couldn't yet trust him, couldn't let herself believe that what he was saying was true.

"She's curled up in the back seat of the black Mustang in the garage, fast asleep."

"That's Greg's car. I should have known she'd hide in a place where she felt safe."

Steven blew out a long breath. "Okay, so I was thinking… Given everything that's been happening, maybe we should get away from all the neighbors and the noise, and discuss what to do next. I'd still like to persuade you to talk to the police. But, for the moment, I suppose that can wait."

THREE

Etta hadn't been behind the wheel of her brother-in-law's Mustang Mach 1 since her sister's funeral. That was three weeks ago, but the memory of that day still burned.

Friends had been invited to stop by the house after the church service, and Greg, knee-deep in grief and denial, had asked her to go out to buy food for the mourners. Of course, she had agreed to make a quick stop at the local grocery store, where it had taken all the fortitude she could muster to make it through the checkout and then load her purchases into the car.

If only she'd known then that her hurried shopping trip would turn out to be the best part of a nightmare day. But she could never have anticipated the scene that waited for her as she pulled up the driveway, just in time to see Greg being led away in handcuffs. All in front of Polly and the dozens of guests arriving for the luncheon.

What if something like that happened today? What if the police showed up in the next few minutes to arrest her for murder?

Impossible, she decided as she buckled her sleeping niece into her booster seat. At this point, no one knew about the intruder. While she had been outside, Steven had moved the man's body into the pantry, where it would be out of sight.

Steeling her nerves, she inched the Mustang down the driveway and past the block party, which was still in full swing. No one gave them a second look as they cruised toward the stop sign, not even the kids playing cornhole in the street. She made a wide arc around the game and then stepped out of the car to push aside the wooden barricade cordoning off the block.

She glanced over at Steven, whose eyes were fixed on his phone. "I wish I could help with directions, but I'm not sure which way to go," she said. "Except for the trip from the airport and a couple of stops at the grocery store, I haven't seen much of the town. Lilly kept inviting me to visit, but I've been working out of Tucson, fifteen-hour shifts with hardly a break. I should have made an effort to get here. But something always seemed to get in the way." The weight of that truth felt heavy on her shoulders. She hadn't spent any time with Lilly in the months before she died.

"Etta?" Steven set the phone on the console and fixed her with a steady glance. "You don't need to explain why you didn't visit your sister as often as you would have liked. I know about the sacrifices you made when Lilly was a teen, so no judgment here."

Of course. Steven had been around for a part of Lilly's awful adolescence. It was embarrassing now to recall how much of their time together had been spent discussing her sister's misbehavior.

"She cleaned up her act, you know," Etta said as she shot a quick glance at Steven. She didn't know why it mattered, but she wanted him to understand that Lilly had grown out of her teenage angst. "When she met Greg, she started reading the Bible and going to church. She walked away from the people that were influencing her bad behavior. And she really became her best self once Polly was born. She had a great part-time job working as a reporter for the local paper. And the last time we talked, she mentioned that she had started to do some freelance work for the *Dallas Observer*. She was hoping it could turn into a regular gig."

"Glad to hear it." He looked at his phone. "I think we should drive downtown. Seems like the best place to find a quiet spot to discuss what to do next."

Etta nodded. She didn't blame Steven for not wanting to talk about Lilly. Her sister had been awful when they'd started dating, doing everything she could to undermine their relationship.

She made a turn, piloting the vehicle through an upscale neighborhood, where signs of the season were everywhere—baskets of geraniums hanging from porch rails, tufts of new grass popping up along the sidewalks and legions of walkers, clad in shorts and T-shirts, enjoying the early summer weather.

"Nice ride!" a group of teenage boys called out, pointing to the Mustang.

"We probably should have taken your car," Etta said, shifting her eyes once again to look at Steven. "Greg's Mustang is attracting way too much attention."

"I took an Uber to your place." He shrugged. "I'm still not driving because of the accident."

She eyed him briefly. "What accident?"

"That's a story that can keep for later. You just need to relax right now. No one is after us."

Etta shifted her focus to the rearview mirror. Steven was right. There were no police cars following behind her, just a tan Suburban, crawling along at barely the speed limit, two car lengths back from the Mustang. Once again, feelings of guilt and remorse threatened to overwhelm her thoughts. She had killed a man. And the fact that she hadn't intended to strike a fatal blow didn't count for much in the reckoning.

"When do you think the kid will wake up?" Steven craned his neck for a view of the back seat.

"I'm not sure. She didn't sleep that well last night, so she's probably exhausted."

Her gaze returned to the mirror. The Suburban had moved up and was now only a dozen or so feet behind them.

"Steven," she said, struggling to hear her own voice over the pounding of her heart. "That tan SUV has been tailing us for a while. The driver is wearing sunglasses and a ball cap, and so is the passenger, so I can't really see their faces. But neither one looks like the gray-bearded guy who talked to me in the yard."

Steven swiveled around to look through the back window. "I see them." He leaned back, holding up his phone. "Smile, guys," he said, snapping their picture. He lined up another quick shot.

Etta took a couple of quick turns without signaling, circling one block and then another, but her serpentine route through the empty streets was not enough to shake the Suburban from their tail.

She tried to tamp down the panic threading through her senses. Maybe the driver really was just a harmless tailgater. But, as the SUV nudged even closer to her bumper, that theory made less and less sense.

She needed to do something…and fast. "Hang on. I have an idea."

Cranking the wheel hard, she took the curve as they veered off Northumberland Drive, blowing through a stop sign as she headed south toward the center of town. She had traveled through the area only once before, in the car with Greg on the way from the airport, and she didn't remember much. But she did have a specific memory of passing a two-level parking garage, adjacent to a municipal building that housed the library and city hall.

She floored the gas pedal, skidding onto the ramp, but was heading the wrong way toward the top level. Just as she had hoped, the angle was too sharp for the SUV. Its tires screeched as the driver overshot the turn.

"Etta." Steven's voice sounded far away.

"I got this," she said.

A quick circle around the upper level, and they headed down the ramp toward the street. It was getting darker now, the once navy sky transformed into a gray backdrop for the tiniest sliver of a moon. She needed to use the shadowy dusk to her advantage. Beside her in the passenger seat, Steven reached back and looped a hand around Polly's car seat. She was still asleep.

"I think you lost them."

"Maybe. But just in case, keep an eye out for a crowded store or fast-food restaurant."

"There's a McDonald's up ahead," Steven said.

Etta veered into the lot, racing at top speed toward the back of the building. She pulled to a stop and cut the lights.

Then, she closed her eyes and said a quick prayer.

Steven released his grip on the car seat and turned back to face the front of the car. "You still okay?"

"Yeah," she said. As okay as she could be after speeding through a parking ramp in the middle of the city.

"Something is clearly going on here, Etta. Something that is too big for us to handle. First, an intruder broke into the house, and now we have two men tailing us through town. We're less than two miles from the police station. What do you say we head there and go in and explain the situation to the authorities?"

"How can I do that when I don't even understand it myself?" Etta slumped against the seat, pushing back the tears that had begun to leak from the corners of her eyes. For so long after her sister's death, she'd done her best to hold it all together, not once breaking down, even on the day of the funeral when Greg was arrested. But this—the prospect of getting arrested and having Polly taken away from her for good—was too much to bear.

"I can't go to jail," she said. "I told Lilly that I'd be here for Polly. That I'd take care of her and love her if anything happened to her or Greg. And something did happen. And now I need to step up and fulfill my promise."

"Okay, Etta." Steven steepled his hand over the screen of his phone. "But let's not take anything off the table until we hash all this out. What do you say we drive along the highway and find a motel? Get a room where Polly can sleep, and we can sit outside and sort through the options."

There was a rustling of movement in the back seat—Polly, awake at last, frowning and confused.

"Hi, sweet pea." Tenderness flooded Etta's tone. "Sorry about all the commotion. But a lot has happened since you fell asleep. This guy in the passenger seat is my friend Steven. He's going to be hanging out with us for a little while. Are you hungry?"

Polly shook her head, which was good since Etta didn't relish the thought of getting stuck in the drive-through and the chance of being spotted by the men in the SUV.

"Okay. Well, let me know if you want something to eat." She had a few fruit bars in her purse, but they were hardly enough to sustain a hungry child. At some point, she'd need to stop at a store, but priority one was convincing Steven that it would be a bad idea to involve the police. And if he didn't agree, she'd drop him off at the bus station and handle the situation on her own.

Steven looked up from the map on his phone. "I found a place that isn't far. I should probably just go ahead and make a reservation."

She exited the lot slowly, looking carefully to the left and the right. But there was no sign of anyone following them. The GPS route led them through the north side of the city, past row after row of homes similar to the one belonging to Greg and Lilly. Etta released a sigh as the Mustang picked up speed, and she put more and more space between them and the last place they'd seen the tan Suburban. Relief flooded her senses. It felt like they had done something bigger than just completing a short drive to reach the outskirts of town. Etta imagined younger versions of herself and Steven bumping fists to celebrate the accomplishment.

Those kinds of moments were all part of the past now, although Etta did allow herself the luxury of a smile. It was a smile that lasted until a neon sign beckoned them toward the weather-beaten canopy shielding the entrance of the Tick Tock Motel.

"It looks pretty crowded," she said, glancing at the number of vehicles parked in the lot.

"Yeah. But crowded could be a good thing. I booked a room under the name of Cassidy Carruthers. That seemed like the best way to go. And old Cassidy has always served me well on the circuit."

Right. Etta cast a sideways glance at Steven. He didn't need to explain why he often used a fake name when he checked into hotels. Because back in the day, as Etta had eventually realized after only a few weeks of spending time with him, when it came to bull riding, Steven Hunt was kind of a big deal. A handsome cowboy with a mop of dark hair tucked under his hat and a lopsided grin that made it clear that he didn't take much in life too seriously. Even now, he was just as handsome as she remembered, maybe even more so now, with the flecks of gray in his beard and the fine laugh lines around those eyes she knew so well from all the time she'd spent staring into them. How had she not recognized him when he first came running through the patio door?

"I have cash, so I'll check us in," she said. "Cassidy is a fairly androgynous name."

Her hands were shaking as she stepped out of the car and walked into the small office at the front of the motel.

Inside, a dark-haired teen behind a plexiglass barrier slid a form through the bottom slot when Etta announced she had a reservation. Etta curled her *C*'s as she signed in as Cassidy Carruthers. Then, she counted out four twenty-dollar bills and set them on the counter. In return, she received change and a key card marked with the number *6*, which, she was told, was to a door at the far end of the L-shaped cluster of rooms on the property.

She shot a quick smile at the girl behind the check-in desk. "Can I grab a couple of toothbrushes and some toothpaste?"

"Sure," the teen said, reaching into a drawer and pulling out a few bags full of often-forgotten essentials. "This okay?"

"Absolutely. Thanks," Etta said, maintaining eye contact as she backed across the room.

Well, that was easy. She had almost made it to the door when a loud voice called out to stop her.

"Wait!" the girl practically shouted. "Something's wrong."

Etta froze in her tracks.

"You didn't fill out the make and license plate of your car. Any vehicle not registered with the office will be towed at the owner's expense."

"Right," Etta said, then muttered under her breath, "Wouldn't want that to happen after everything else today."

Steven's eyes blinked open, and he stared in confusion around the small room. An illuminated clock displayed the time—6:02 a.m. But where was he? And why were both his back and jaw throbbing? His limbs felt leaden, as if he'd been run over by a bulldozer. And more than anything, he wished he could go back to sleep. But after growing up on a ranch, the routine of waking up at six to complete chores was ingrained in his very core. He stretched his arms and realized he wasn't in a bed, but rather, was slumped in a chair. His eyes adjusted to the dim light, and he spotted the other two people sharing the space, both still asleep in a double bed. Ah. Right. The events from the previous day flashed across his brain. The long bus ride down from Dallas. The Uber to Dogwood Drive. The sight of Etta lying on the floor and the fight with the intruder. The harried search for Polly and the drive out of town.

He reached up to gingerly touch his jaw. It was definitely swollen, and probably black and blue, too. Good thing he was keeping his beard longer these days. Maybe no one would notice that he looked a bit worse for wear. The small motel room felt safe enough, but he had pushed the one chair against the door, just in case. And, truth be told, it wasn't the most uncomfortable place he'd ever spent the night. A soft chair beat a horse stall and a bale of hay any day. But, between all of his injuries, old and new, his body was sure feeling tender.

He glanced again at the bed. Dark brown hair spilled across a white pillow as Etta slept on her side, holding Polly against her chest. Etta was still as beautiful as she'd ever been, yet at the same time so different from the girl he'd known all those years ago.

Don't go there. The rational part of his brain blinked out a warning, but he was already gone. Back to that dusty road where he had pulled his truck over and tried to change Etta's mind about breaking their engagement. But she had been adamant, her *no* as sure as the *yes* she'd uttered just one day earlier, when she'd accepted his ring.

A twelve-hour engagement after a two-month courtship. Crazy to even think of that today. He and Etta had been on a roller-coaster ride filled with dips and turns from the moment they'd met to their last, angry argument, when she'd told him that rather than getting married, she wanted to work as a traveling nurse. Oh, she had her ambitions. Thinking back, he had to admire her drive. That girl had been fiery and fiercely independent, with big plans for her life—plans to get out of Texas and see the world. That girl had been biding her time, waiting for her kid sister to finish high school before she set off on her grand adventure.

But the Etta he'd met yesterday seemed like a different person. Part of it was superficial. She was wearing her hair longer now, and the bangs that used to hang down into her dark brown eyes and frame her open face had grown out. It made her seem more grown-up, more mature. Which, of course, she was. They both were. Fifteen years was a long time. But it was the worry in her eyes and the anxiety that tightened her face that had caught him by surprise. Twenty-one-year-old Etta hadn't had an easy childhood, but she'd always seemed fearless and impervious to the harsher realities of life. The Etta of today still radiated that same courage, but now there was a new layer of vulnerability.

He pushed his hands through his hair. If he had noticed changes in Etta, what must she have thought of him? She hadn't even recognized him when he'd shown up at the house. He knew all too well that his boyish good looks were long gone. Every day he grimaced at the stranger in the mirror—a stranger with deep lines around his eyes and threads of gray in his hair and beard, both of which needed to be trimmed.

He stifled a groan and pulled himself to his feet. It was time to stop stalling and face the morning. Don't Delay! Seize the Day! had been one of his dad's favorite mottos growing up. While it had certainly annoyed him when he had been an exhausted teen, trying to catch up on sleep, he had grown to appreciate the sentiment.

Last night had not gone the way he had hoped. He had imagined them putting Polly down in one of the beds, and then pulling up chairs outside the room so they could finally talk. He had it all planned out—what he would say to make her see that running away was the absolutely worst thing to do, how he would convince her that turning herself in to the police was the only logical course of action left open, given the circumstances.

But that conversation was put on the back burner as Polly fussed, thrusting her little body to and fro on the bed until Etta had agreed to lie down next to her. Moments later, they were both asleep.

But, hey, this was a new day. When Etta woke up, they could still have that talk while Polly holed up inside, watching cartoons. Maybe he could persuade her to turn herself in to the police. But first, coffee.

Stiffness shortened his steps as he pushed the chair away from the door and then quietly unlatched the lock. Sunshine was already streaming down against the parking lot as he stepped outside, his eyes squinting as he stared at the still-full lot. Last night, there were no parking spots in the front, so Etta had pulled around to the back lot.

A red Dodge Charger he hadn't noticed last night was parked in front of the main office. It was kind of early for check-in, and his gut instincts snapped to full alert. He pulled his worn ball cap out of his back pocket and tugged it down low on his head. His clothes were wrinkled from being slept in all night, but this motel didn't seem like it would stand on ceremony.

He pulled open the door to the office and walked toward the large urns of coffee, set out on a long table. The small room felt cramped, even though it was mostly empty. A family of four was sitting at one of the tables, two children eating cereal while their parents watched the news on TV. Two thirtysomething men were standing beside the check-in counter, drumming their fingers impatiently. There was no sign of the teenager who had checked them in the night before.

He pushed down on the lever and filled one cup with piping hot liquid, then fitted on a lid. He picked up a second cup and looked around. He took his coffee black, but, if he remembered correctly, Etta liked a splash of milk. Ah. The milk was over by the cereal. He quickly filled the cup and then carried the steaming drink over to the counter with the food.

"Hey," one of the men suddenly said.

Steven glanced over at them. An older man with curly red hair had appeared behind the counter and was offering a quizzical smile. "Are you here to check in? It's early, but we might be able to make accommodations."

"Nah, we don't want to stay at your motel. We're looking for someone. Or rather, a couple of someones who are in trouble with the law."

The hairs on the back of Steven's neck stood up. He finished pouring milk into the coffee, struggling to maintain an air of nonchalance as he took a few steps closer to the counter so he could hear the rest of the conversation and get a better look at the two men. He couldn't be sure if they were the driver and passenger of the tan SUV that had followed them yesterday through town. If so, they had probably changed cars. They were dressed almost identically, in pastel polo shirts and tan khakis. Both had short dark hair worn in a buzz cut. The one in the light blue shirt stepped closer to the counter and continued taking charge of the situation.

"Yeah," he said. "Can you tell me if you had a youngish woman check in last night with a small child? There may have a been someone else with them, too."

"Oh, I am sorry, but I can't give out information about our guests. Besides, I wasn't working the evening shift yesterday."

The skinnier of the two men reached into his pocket and pulled out a thick wad of bills.

"Listen. We're in kind of a hurry here. That's our car parked out front, and we're anxious to get back on the road. I understand your reluctance, but this is very important. Is there any way that I could maybe make it worth your while?"

The proprietor stared at the cash for a beat and then nodded. "Let me get my daughter. She handles all of the late check-ins. Maybe she can help."

FOUR

Steven's first instinct was to rush back to the room, wake up Etta and Polly, jump in the car and get back on the road. But the inquisitive side of him wanted more information. Neither man had a gray beard like the guy Etta had encountered in the yard, but there was something about the thinner one that was oddly familiar. Steven took out his phone and pulled up the photo he'd taken the day before. It was hard to be certain, since both men had been wearing sunglasses and ball caps, but they could easily be the ones standing at the counter less than five feet away from him.

They had claimed to be looking for someone in trouble with the law, but neither had flashed a badge. Instead, they had offered a bribe. Not cops, then.

How much time did he have before the proprietor of the motel returned with his daughter? Two minutes? Five minutes? Still, if he could cause a distraction, maybe he could buy them some time to make their escape. His eyes scanned the small space again.

A buffet crammed with prepackaged breakfast foods—cereal, muffins, yogurt— and a stack of paper plates. Nothing useful. Then there were the coffee dispensers on the other side of the room. No help there, either.

Frustration pumped through his veins. If he was going to do something, he needed to act fast. He had already wasted precious seconds when he could be back at the motel room, warning Etta and packing the car. He turned on his heel, preparing to walk out the door, when his gaze fell upon something he had missed. An idea began to form in his mind. It was a long shot, but then again, wasn't he the king of long shots? Sure, his return to rodeo hadn't gone quite as planned, but that just meant he was due some success this time around. And if this move didn't work, then he would just head out of the office and hurry Etta and Polly on their way.

He trained his eyes toward the ceiling of the small room. No cameras. Good. If what he was about to do was to succeed long-term, he didn't want to leave any video evidence.

These guys were smart. They'd found the motel before twelve hours had passed. The main advantage he and Etta had was the fact that the men were unaware of Steven's identity. He moved just a few feet to the side, then edged closer to the family having their breakfast, as the youngest son—a little boy of about four—approached the table with a full glass of orange juice.

Steven stepped forward and deliberately nudged his arm, causing the little boy to drop the plastic cup and sending a spray of liquid onto Steven's pants. "Whoa. Watch it there," Steven said as he tripped backward, stumbling against one of the two men, who were still waiting by the counter. Too late, the dad of the family cried out a warning, and that resulted in the little boy to bursting into tears.

The motel owner came hurrying back down the stairs without his daughter. There was a flurry of excitement and apologies. But, within in a matter of seconds, the tumult died away. Steven bent down to console the crying child, hoping to keep the men from seeing through his ploy. But the evasion wasn't necessary. Their only reaction was to pester the proprietor about his daughter's whereabouts.

"She'll be here in five minutes. I told her

that you were looking for information, and she said she'd come down here as soon as she can." Now the motel owner seemed far more concerned with wiping up all the spilled orange juice than appeasing the grumbling men.

That was Steven's cue to make his exit. With a final apology to the family, he headed out the door, his hands jammed into his pockets. His theatrics seemed to have worked, and no one seemed to suspect his stumble hadn't been orchestrated to pick the pocket of the man waiting by the counter. A smile curled on his lips. Some people looked down on rodeo folks, and sure, there were plenty of sketchy characters. Heck, he'd been one of them at seventeen. One good scolding from his mama when she'd found his collection of stolen keychains had put an end to his life of crime, and he'd never lifted anything again. Until now.

He pulled his own key fob out of his pocket and slipped open the blade of the small Swiss Army knife attached by a link. Then, just like he was out for a stroll through the parking lot, he sidled up next to the Charger and plunged the knife into the front tire.

He waited until he heard the satisfying hiss

of air and then he continued on his way. Once he reached the motel room, he flashed his keycard to unlock the door.

The space was still dim as he stepped inside, but both Etta and Polly were sitting up in bed. His heart thumped as Etta, her hair matted down on one side and her face still soft and relaxed from sleep, offered him a smile. No one should look that good after such a stressful day. But, then again, Etta always looked good. It was part of her charm.

"We have to hit the road immediately," he said as he set down the coffee, then scrambled around to collect their stuff. Etta didn't bother asking him any questions, but sprang out of the rumpled bed, pulling Polly with her.

"We're going back into the car now, sweetie." Her voice was calm as she spoke to the little girl. But already, the fine lines of worry were back as her jaw seemed to tighten.

Her gaze met his. "Problems?"

"Nothing we can't handle. There are two men at the front office asking questions. But since we parked in the back lot, they don't know which room we're in. Yet. We have to hurry."

Etta swept up the few items she had brought

along for Polly as Steven opened the door a few inches and looked toward the office. No signs of the men yet. But their car was still parked in front.

He waited a moment and then checked outside again. Still clear.

"You and Polly start walking to the car while I keep a lookout."

Etta gave him a worried glance, but he shook his head. This wasn't the time to dwell on the negative. For now, their focus had to be on escape. The next time he glanced through the crack, Etta and Polly had turned the corner toward the back of the motel and were out of sight. Time for him to start moving. He stepped across the threshold, his eyes tracking the entrance to the motel. When he reached the edge of the building, he sprinted toward the back lot.

His chest hurt from the short jog to the car, but he tried to cover up how winded he was as he pulled open the passenger door.

He slid in. "Ready to go?"

Etta nodded as she pulled forward and drove to the far end of the lot. "Highway or back roads?"

He turned his head for a final view of the motel entrance. The men were standing on the front pavement, looking down at the Charger's flat tire. "Let's take the interstate down two exits, and then hop off the main road. I'll map out a route on my phone."

He pulled out his cell as Etta merged onto the highway. A quick glance behind him confirmed that no one was following them.

"Hey! We did it!" He gave Etta a smile. "Good thing you're not high-maintenance, or we might not have beat them."

But Etta didn't smile at the joke. Her fingers were curled around the steering wheel and her lips were pressed tight.

"Who are these people?" she asked. "And how did they find us?"

The same thought had been tumbling around in his own head. Not for the first time, he wished his twin brother, Seb, was here. As sheriff of their county up in South Dakota, his brother would have the resources to help them. "I have a few ideas about how they managed to track us down. But as to who they are? I'm not sure, but I might know a way we can find out."

Etta cast a glance in his direction. "How is that?"

"Well, when I first started working the rodeo, I went through a slight delinquent phase. I wasn't going to church, and, well, I acted like the rules didn't apply to me anymore since I was living as an adult. I had a friend who worked the sideshows at the rodeo. And he taught me some of his tricks. Long story short—" he reached into his pocket and pulled out the wallet he'd lifted from the burlier of the two men "—we might be able to get some answers from this."

Etta pulled in a deep breath. She had hardly recovered from yesterday, and now, once again, they were on the run, fleeing for their lives from men who seemed to have superhuman tracking abilities.

A shiver started at her shoulders and ran down her spine as the reality of their situation dawned on her. What would have happened if Steven hadn't been in the motel office when their pursuers arrived? She and Polly might be dead.

Just like Lilly.

"Hey! Look at that!" Etta shook off the feelings of fear and anxiety and pointed toward a rainbow arcing over the horizon. It was the perfect reminder that she needed to keep her focus on hope and trust in her Creator, even during the darkest times.

A rustling movement drew her attention to the back seat as Polly leaned forward, a deep frown etched across her lips.

"Did you see the rainbow, Pol?" Etta asked.

Polly nodded.

"Is there something you want me to do?"

Another nod as Polly pointed to a disc wedged next to the console on which Lilly had written Favorite Hymns.

"Shall we give it a listen?" Etta asked.

Another nod. Etta pushed the CD into the slot on the player and music filled the car.

Steven was quick to identify the song. "'How Great Thou Art,'" he said.

"Lilly's favorite." Etta smiled. "They played it at her wedding." For a moment, she was transported to the small back room of the restaurant where they had gone to celebrate after the ceremony. Her sister had been so radiant that day, joyful and excited at the prospect of a new life ahead. Etta sucked in a long breath as guilt seeped into her memories. With Lilly happily married, Etta had taken a step back in their relationship, visiting once or twice a year, calling every couple of months to catch up on all the moments she was missing. New house, new job, new baby. She had listened as her sister talked about her

jam-packed days and the challenges of raising Polly. Lilly's newfound confidence had
offered Etta a reason to pull back, to be less
involved in her sister's life. At the time, Etta
had been grateful for the break. Now, she was
filled with regret.

When the song ended, she ejected the disc
and turned back toward her niece. "Your
mama sure did love that one. I remember her
singing it to you after you were born."

Polly smiled as she settled back in her seat.

Etta shifted her eyes toward Steven and
said lowly, "Maybe it's a leap, but I think
she knew I was fretting and wanted to cheer
me up."

He nodded. "Well, she picked a good song."

"She did. So…what next?"

"Well. Let's see if the contents of this wallet will provide a few answers about the men
from the motel." Steven flipped open the billfold and looked inside. "Apparently, the owner's name is Matt Bickler, age…" He slid the
ID out of the plastic and squinted. "Thirty-
four. Dallas address. Ring any bells?"

"I'm not sure. The name does sound
slightly familiar."

He pulled out his phone and began to type.
A moment later, he looked up and said, "I

found a Matt Bickler. Attorney with the firm Thompson, Colfax and Bickler."

Of course…that was where she knew the name. "Greg's lawyer is Sam Colfax. Odd coincidence, don't you think?"

He took a moment to compare pictures. "It's the same guy. And *odd* is hardly the word for it." Steven shuffled through the remaining items in the wallet. "Credit card. Gym membership. Sticker for that guy who's running for reelection as Texas attorney general. Oh, and hey, look at this. Apparently, he's a customer at Pizza Roundup. Two more punches and he'll earn a free pie."

Etta turned again to face Steven. "How do you think they found us?"

"Most likely they pinged your phone. I turned it off when we got into the car, but it's possible that they're tracking the Mustang. I know you don't want to hear it, but I need to say it again. This is a job for the police."

Etta shook her head. "I've already explained why going to the police is not an option. Is there a plan B?"

Steven shot her a look. "Not really. Not if you want to keep Polly safe. Continuing to run is a huge mistake."

"But what if there was a way we could stay

off the radar? I don't trust the police to handle this right. And the fact that Greg's lawyer is a partner of one of the men following us is troublesome, to say the least." Could she even trust Greg? Why was someone from the law firm representing him after them? Deep down, she knew Greg wouldn't do anything to harm his family—certainly not Polly. "Maybe the next step is to talk to Greg and see if he can fill in some blanks about the situation."

Steven frowned. "Etta, no. That's not a good idea. And I have to ask—what's the endgame in all of this? I thought the goal here was protecting Polly."

"This *is* all part of that goal. We don't know who we can trust yet. I'd like to ask Greg a few questions."

"Consider this as an alternative." Steven seemed to be having a hard time hiding his exasperation. "You asked about a plan B. How about we head north to my family's ranch in South Dakota? My brother, Seb, is the sheriff there, and he can help us look into your sister's case."

Huh. During their long-ago courtship, she had heard a lot of stories about Steven's twin brother, but she didn't know he was a sheriff. But as interesting as that was, she still didn't think it was good idea to involve Steven's family in her personal problems. She had killed someone and fled a crime scene. It all just seemed too risky.

She looked at Steven and shook her head. "The last thing I want to do is put your family in danger by asking them to shelter me and Polly."

"I'm one-hundred-percent certain that they'd want to help. But, if it makes you feel better, I can call and run the idea by them before we show up on their doorstep."

"It's a kind offer. But before we do anything, I'd still like to discuss all of this with Greg. This situation with his lawyer is so sketchy. Sam Colfax and Matt Bickler could be leading Greg down a rabbit hole that would make it impossible for him to prove his innocence or for there to be justice for Lilly." She couldn't run away if there was a chance of that happening. She wanted justice for her sister as much as she wanted to protect her niece.

Steven sighed. "Well, whatever we decide, we're going to need to ditch this car as soon as possible. I'm just thinking out loud here, but I'd say that the best place to do that would be at the airport. We can leave the Mustang in the long-term lot and rent a new vehicle to drive to South Dakota."

"With a quick stop afterward at the prison," Etta persisted.

The landscape got bleaker and bleaker as they headed north, toward the airport. Tall scrub grass leaned down by the side of the road. The drought had been hard on this part of the county, and the farmers had to be looking for some much-needed rain.

But just that quickly, the freshly plowed fields gave way to a more suburban landscape as they reached the outskirts of the big city.

"I just thought of something," Etta said. She'd been too distracted to think of it before. "You can't rent a car without a license, and it's probably risky for me to do it in my name."

Steven glanced at her. "What makes you think I don't have a license?" Steven shuffled through the cards in his wallet. "Actually, I have three. One in my name, one for Cassidy Carruthers and the last one courtesy of Matt Bickler."

"I thought you said you couldn't drive."

He raised an eyebrow. "How have you not

heard about this? It was on the news, and it was featured in a four-page spread in *People*."

"I've been busy," she said defensively. "And since when was there national interest in something that happened at a rodeo?"

There was a long pause.

"Okay, fine," she said, fighting the urge to roll her eyes. "I'm guessing you got wrecked again in the ring. Was it worse than what happened the first time we met?"

He shrugged. "Nah. Not nearly that bad. Just enough to sideline me for the season."

"Hmm." Etta pressed her lips together, unsure of whether or not to believe him. Steven had always been a little reckless. "How long ago did this take place?"

He ran a hand across his beard. "End of February."

"And you still can't drive?"

"Okay, counselor," he said, raising his hands in a gesture of surrender. "You are correct that my injuries were a bit worse than I've been letting on. But can we ease off on the interrogation just a bit? Because none of that matters in light of the rest of this stuff that's going on."

She let the subject drop, at least for the moment. Following the signs, Etta parked the

Mustang in the airport's long-term lot and helped load their gear on a luggage cart. Now that she was paying attention, she noticed that Steven was walking with a decided limp, and she resolved to find out what had happened in February.

After a fifteen-minute shuttle ride, they reached the rental-car center. So far, so good. But once inside, they were faced with a choice of more than ten companies offering a variety of packages and a selection of different vehicles. Security cameras were everywhere, and Etta's eyes locked on one particular revolving lens with a wide-angle view. Steven must have noticed it, too, because he stepped sideways to avoid getting tagged in the picture.

An intercom crackled with announcements as they made their way toward the line in front of the Hertz rental counter. "We don't have a reservation, so this might take a while," Steven said. "You two grab a seat. I'll try to be as quick as I can."

Etta pointed to a row of chairs by a window. "We'll wait for you over there." She tugged at Polly's hand, but the little girl refused to move. Her lower lip trembled, and her eyes filled with tears.

"Would you like to ride in the baggage cart while I go get our car?" Steven asked.

Polly nodded.

He turned to Etta. "Will you help me get her up here?"

"Of course." Her gaze tracked Steven's efforts as he bent to lift Polly. The cowboy she had known so long ago had been wiry and fit. But the rough life of the circuit had taken its toll on his body. And that last injury must have been a lot worse than he was letting on.

Etta found a quiet corner where she could wait. Polly's face remained impassive as Etta tried to explain what was going on. She had gotten quite adept at making up stories centered around the small details of home life, but it wouldn't do to mention that they would soon be headed to the prison to see Polly's dad. Every so often, she glanced at her watch. As the minutes ticked by, it became harder and harder to understand the delay. Finally, Steven ambled over to join them, smiling as he led them through a dark parking lot toward a blue minivan.

Polly's forehead wrinkled as she pointed to the van and shook her head.

Steven bent to reassure her. "Don't worry, kid. It's only a loaner. Your dad's car will be here, waiting for him here when he comes home. Until then, this will be more comfortable for all of us, but especially for our new friend." He pulled open the sliding door to reveal a small stuffed rabbit perched on the back seat. "He looked kind of lonely, and I was hoping he could hang out with you for a little while."

Polly's smile was pure sunshine. Grinning, she climbed up and settled back against her car seat. Then, after snapping the safety strap into the clip, she put on her headphones and pulled her bunny close to her chest.

Etta slid into the driver's seat, and Steven handed her the keys. "When did you find the time to shop for that?"

He grinned. "You're not going to believe it. The guy behind me in line saw me talking to Polly. He had bought the rabbit at the airport gift shop for his niece, but he must have realized that Polly needed it more than she did. Nice guy."

The gesture, from both Steven and the stranger, touched her heart. "Absolutely. So, next stop, the prison?"

He pulled in a deep breath.

"I don't think we have a choice here, Steven. It's actually a practical solution if you think about it. Greg could have some information that will help us keep Polly safe."

"Fine...but I'm going to be the one who goes inside." She was about to protest when he held up a hand. "I know that you're convinced of your brother-in-law's innocence, but with his law firm being involved in all this, I'd like to get a read on him myself. Besides, the police are probably looking for you, and, so far, anyway, I've been staying off the radar. The only hitch will be if Greg refuses to see me because he doesn't recognize my name."

Etta bit down hard on her lip, recalling what her sister thought of Steven Hunt. "He's heard of you, of course," she said diplomatically. "But maybe not in a good way."

Steven met and held her glance. "Glad to know. Do you have a set time when you talk to him each week?"

Etta snuck a peek at her niece in the middle seat. Since the headrests were thick and high enough to muffle most sound, even if Polly slipped off her headphones, it was unlikely she could hear what was being discussed in the front. Still, Etta lowered her voice as she turned toward Steven.

"He calls when he can, but it's usually

about Polly. Before he was arrested, he and I talked about getting Polly in to see a counselor in the hope that she might open up about what happened when Lilly was killed. It's possible—likely, in fact—that she saw something the day of the murder. It happened in the morning, and Polly was home at the time, so she might have been there when the killer came to the door." Etta still shuddered to think about her little niece, terrified and worried about her mother. "But what exactly she witnessed, we don't know. Greg tried to talk to her about it, of course, and so did the police. I tried as well. But you've seen how it is. She just won't speak."

Steven frowned, his countenance grim. "I suppose it would explain why Polly has become a target. Poor kid. I can't imagine how difficult that would be for her if she was, in fact, a witness to her mother's murder."

Etta turned her head to the side and pushed back tears. Everything had happened so fast that there had been barely time to formulate a plan to help Polly deal with the sadness and confusion of her mother's death. Her cheeks were wet when she turned back to face Steven.

"I can't even think about it without breaking down. Polly has been through so much. I know she misses Lilly, but she misses Greg, too. That's one of the reasons to talk to him. Maybe there's something he can tell us that will help put an end to all of this."

Steven sighed. "Fine. But let's just not get our hopes up, okay?" He paused for a moment. "I just had an idea that might be a game changer. While I was waiting in line at the rental counter, I took another look at Matt Bickler's license. He and I are close to the same age and build, give or take a few inches. The main difference is that Bickler looks like a hipster rock star, and I look like…" He shrugged. "Me. But with a little help from a razor and some bleach, I think I could do a fairly good impersonation. Greg might agree to see me if he thought I was affiliated with his law firm. And masquerading as Matt Bickler will allow me to keep my real identity hidden for the time being."

As ideas went, it wasn't the worst. This way, neither of them would be spotted at the prison while trying to lie low. But a lot would be riding on Steven's ability to assume a false identity. "But what if the guards at the prison see through your disguise?"

"We'll cross that bridge when we come to it. But we should talk about something before I meet with your brother-in-law. Are you positive that he had nothing to do with your sister's murder?"

Etta nodded. A twinge of doubt poked at her, but she pushed it away. "I know the facts don't line up in Greg's favor, but I can't see him deliberately trying to hurt Lilly in any way."

"Okay, then. We should move forward on that assumption. But we need to keep an open mind and not view anything as a given. And once we finish up at the prison, we'll set the GPS for the ranch in South Dakota."

FIVE

Visiting Greg would have to wait. First up was perfecting Steven's transformation into Matt Bickler.

"Second exit and turn left," Steven said, reading the directions to Walmart on his phone.

"Got it," Etta said. She wasn't completely sold on the idea of Steven disguising himself to gain entrance to the prison. But he had insisted that it would be too risky for her to take the lead on this. And though he didn't say so directly, she suspected that he wanted to make his own decision about her brother-in-law's involvement in Lilly's death.

"I've used an alias countless times when I was out on the circuit, and no one questioned me at all."

"But Cassidy Carruthers is you, just with a different name. This time, you're pretending to be someone completely different, both in appearance and in mannerisms. That's a big enough challenge. But what if Greg has met Matt Bickler and knows what he looks like? He won't be fooled by bleached hair and a pair of hipster glasses."

Steven waved off that possibility. "I'm not concerned. One guy with short, spiky hair looks like a dozen others. Even if their paths did cross at some point, Greg wouldn't have been focused on details. Panic does crazy things to the psyche. Consider the fact that you didn't recognize me when you saw me at your sister's house. That took me down a few pegs."

"But…"

"Stop worrying, Etta. You need to trust that I can do this, okay?"

Etta bit back a sigh and trained her focus on the road ahead.

Even after all the changes of the past fifteen years, Steven still had an extremely healthy ego. Could he really be offended that she'd failed to recognize him at first glance? Given the fact that she was being beaten by her assailant, she might be excused for not rolling out the welcome mat to greet an old friend. And then, of course, once again, the efficient file system of her brain easily turned up another example of Steven's self-centeredness—there was his shocked reaction when he discovered she hadn't been following his accomplishments on the rodeo circuit. What was that all about? Had *he* been following *her* career?

Not likely.

Though to be fair, her work as a traveling nurse didn't garner headlines in the national media. So she supposed he had a point there. But she really had been busy, stuck in an endless cycle of work, sleep, repeat. She could almost hear Steven's retort, that her singlemindedness had always been the root of her problems.

Was that true? She worked hard at her job, which was often gut-wrenchingly sad and always challenging. Etta had to constantly deal with illness and tragedy—being a nurse certainly didn't involve spending evenings out with pals from the circuit.

"Here's our exit, straight ahead." Steven's voice pulled her out of the imaginary argument she was having with herself. An argument that, sad to say, she seemed to be losing. If nothing else, she prided herself on being self-aware.

She flicked on her signal and made the turn toward the Walmart, looming in a half-acre lot straight ahead. A quick glance toward the passenger seat took in Steven's strained countenance and brought a sudden realization that maybe the past few years hadn't been all fun and games for him, either. There had to be more to the story about the most recent injury to his leg.

"What did happen the last time you rode in the ring? Did you pull an ornery bull that no one could handle?"

He shook his head. "Nothing like that. I actually stayed on for the whole eight seconds, and my dismount was sweet, if I do say so myself."

"And then…" she pressed.

He raised a brow. "A buddy got thrown, and I jumped in to help him. His bull didn't like that, and he showed his displeasure by trampling on my leg."

"Oh, Steven." Her voice quavered as she thought about how much that must have hurt. But he shook off her sympathy with a shake of his head.

"It hurt at the time, but it's much better now."

Once they parked and went inside the store,

Steven turned to face her, his eyes bright with anticipation.

"I'm going to check out the hair dyes and then look for some clothes to complete my disguise. You should pick up some things for you and Polly. And also shop for groceries." He waved her toward the grocery aisles. "Once I get the stuff I need, I'll head into one of the private family bathrooms and bleach my hair. We'll keep this stop as quick as possible and then meet at the front so that I can pay."

"But first, shouldn't we…" she began, but then, with a wave and a wink, Steven disappeared into a crowd of shoppers waiting to check out in the front of the store.

Classic. That move captured Steven in a nutshell. One minute, humble about his past heroics; cocky, the next.

Etta's brain flashed back to those early days when she was working the night shift at the hospital, a new nurse with no seniority but plenty of dedication when it came to her patients. She had a special interest in the cowboy she had helped, however briefly, when he'd been hurt in the ring at the country fair. Steven had been pretty out of it after a complicated surgery to repair a punctured lung, a lacerated liver and to set more than a dozen broken bones. But when she had stopped by his hospital room to see how he was doing, he had opened his eyes and immediately shot her a crooked smile.

"Here you are again. Tell me, what did I do right to get the best-looking nurse in the hospital?"

She had smiled back at him. Flirting with patients was frowned upon by the administration, but what was she expected to do when the patient was flirting with her?

He was good-looking and charming. And back then, he was different in every way from most of the guys she knew. Serious and light-hearted at the same time. And supremely self-assured. He was a twin, he told her, the child of a happy family who all still lived on a ranch in South Dakota. Her polar opposite in so many ways.

She had liked him immediately.

Although, that was fifteen years ago. A lot had changed since then. For both of them. Even though she hadn't been following Steven's bull-riding career lately, she knew enough to understand that the sport had been good to him, at least when it came to paying the bills. But maybe not so much in terms of the toll it had taken on his body. That limp looked pretty serious, even as he had moved through the crowd, away from her and Polly. She made another mental note to herself to look into the circumstances of his latest injuries.

"C'mon, Polly," she said, shaking herself out of her reverie. "Let's go find some carrots for your new rabbit. After we get the groceries we need, we'll have plenty of time to look at the clothes and the books."

With a firm grasp on Polly's hand, Etta pushed her cart toward the fruits and vegetables. There, she sifted through bags of apples and oranges, marveling at the freshness of the display. It had been weeks since she had been in a proper grocery store. While staying at the house, she had arranged to have most of their groceries delivered, often dealing with surprising substitutions. The knowledge that today Steven was paying the bill made her more extravagant than usual as she added a bunch of bananas and a large chunk of cheddar cheese to the growing pile of items in her cart.

Soon, they had everything they needed for the days ahead, including two new outfits for Polly and a pair of jeans and a couple of T-shirts for herself. Etta checked her phone and glanced around for Steven. They should have time to quickly check the books.

She was pleased to see that an ample number of picture books filled the shelves, all suitable to the taste and ability level of a precocious five-year-old girl. She hovered near Polly as her niece checked out the selection, taking a moment to eye a display of current bestsellers for herself. She had always enjoyed a good mystery, and she scanned the covers for one that was not too cozy but not too grisly. A difficult balance to find, for sure. But who was she kidding? It wasn't like she was going on a vacation to the islands. There would be little time for reading in the days ahead.

With Polly still looking at books as she sat cross-legged on the floor, Etta's eyes flitted to the bank of TVs along the back wall, and a gasp stuck in her throat as a picture of Greg and Lilly's house flashed across a half-dozen screens. What followed were photos of Etta and Lilly, taken years ago, before Lilly's marriage, with text underneath providing close captions. *Police continue to investigate an apparent homicide in Silver Creek in the four hundred block of Dogwood Drive. Still miss-*

ing is five-year-old Polly Sanderson, who had been left in the care of her aunt, Etta Mitchell...

Etta had seen enough. She grabbed Polly's hand and headed for the front of the store.

Steven ran his fingers through his now-buzzed hair as he caught his reflection in the bathroom mirror. Well, he might not look exactly like Matt Bickler, but he sure didn't resemble himself anymore. Gone were his trademark dark hair and ever-present stubble, which had grown out into a fuller beard of late. He probably hadn't been truly clean-shaven like this since his twin brother's wedding a few years back. It would be good to get to the ranch and see Seb and and his wife, Tacy, again, even though it would mean asking his twin for a pretty big favor. But it wouldn't hurt to have the full force of the law on their side sooner rather than later, given the ruthlessness of the men who were after Etta and Polly.

He studied the picture of Matt Bickler again and fitted the clear glasses he'd purchased on his nose. The green tortoiseshell frames didn't exactly match the ones Matt Bickler was wearing in his picture, but they had the same hipster vibe. And, best of all, they hid the bruises from his earlier fight.

Satisfied, he exited the bathroom in search of Etta. The brown dress shoes pinched a bit and the new pants felt even tighter as he headed for the front of the store.

He spotted Etta. "Excuse me, miss," he said, tapping her on the shoulder.

He had expected a good reaction. Maybe a burst of laughter. Certainly, a smirk and an eye roll. What he had not anticipated was for Etta to flinch away from his touch and shrink into herself.

Or the look of fear as she turned to face him.

It felt like a sucker punch to the gut.

"Etta, it's me. Steven."

She blinked up at him, and then she seemed to pull herself up as understanding flickered.

First, her eyes narrowed and she took a step back, her gaze roaming from the brown tips of his tasseled dress loafers up to the tucked-in metallic shirt and ending at his bleached hair. Her lips quirked, and her eyebrows rose. Steven shifted back and forth, feeling just a bit uncomfortable under her scrutiny. But then, as if a bubble of mirth had risen up from her diaphragm, Etta's mouth curved into a perfect smile. A second later, she doubled over, her entire body shaking with laughter.

"Hey now, it's not that funny." Steven tried to make his voice sound gruff, but he was beaming in her direction. He was happy to lighten her mood, if only for the moment.

He turned to Polly, who was looking at him with her usual gaze of dubious skepticism. "Do you think I look ridiculous? See, Etta, the kid thinks I look as handsome as ever."

Etta pulled in a gulp of air. "Sorry. Sorry. Honestly, I'm impressed. It's just that you usually seem so…" She paused as if trying to think of the right word.

"Good-looking? Manly?" he ventured.

"Rugged," Etta offered. "And this—" she gestured toward his clothing "—well, this is different."

He smirked. Rugged. That seemed like a compliment. He'd take it. For sure. "You ready, then? I already paid for all my stuff, and I even remembered to pick up a couple of burner phones in case we need them. But let's check out your gear and get going. What's with the ball cap, by the way?"

At the mention of her hat, Etta blanched. And, just like that, all the joy on her face evaporated, replaced by pinched anxiety.

"Lilly's house is on the news," she said lowly. "Which means they found the body. No big surprise there, I suppose. But they have a picture of me. It's an old one, but it won't be long before they find one that's more up-to-date. The police are going to be looking for me now. And they'll probably arrest me and take me to jail."

"We'll figure this out before that happens, Etta."

"How can you know that for sure?"

He couldn't, and that was the problem. Twenty years ago, he would have given vent to his feelings with some choice words. But he wasn't a delinquent teen anymore. And he knew that there was only one thing to do when the road became difficult. One person to seek. *God, please give us guidance. Help me to know how to help Etta and Polly and make this right.*

"I'll take Polly and finish up here while you head to the car," he said, as he guided Etta toward the exit door.

Etta nodded and pointed to her hat. "I haven't paid for this yet," she said.

He reached over and ripped off the tag. "Keep it on for now. I'll ring it up at the register," he said, then he watched her walk out the door.

Steven raked his fingers through his hair. Two minutes ago, he had been reveling in the absurdity of his altered appearance. Now, the feel of the spiky strands just served as a reminder of the impossible situation they were in. No, *impossible* wasn't the right word. Challenging. Unexpected. Scary.

For some reason, he hadn't expected the police to be looking for Etta this quickly. What had he been thinking suggesting that she and Polly accompany him into Walmart? Stupid mistake on his part. He pushed any lingering questions out of his brain as he went to the checkout counter. He passed the health and beauty aisle on the way, and on a whim, he grabbed a second box of hair color, this one for Etta. It seemed like a good idea to buy it just in case. He snuck a glance at Polly. Her gaze seemed fixed on a display of Doritos on an end cap. He grabbed a bag and tossed it into the cart. It wasn't the healthiest snack, but the kid deserved a treat.

Steven self-scanned and then bagged the items Etta had selected. He wasn't surprised at her choices. Frugality had always been Etta's way. He could still remember her look of horror the first, and only, time he'd tried to take her to a fancy restaurant, where the entrées ran fifty or sixty dollars a person. He'd been trying to impress her, and instead she had insisted on ordering a salad.

He pulled out his credit card, paid, and then he and Polly headed out the door. Etta was waiting in the van. As he loaded the groceries into the trunk, she buckled Polly into her booster seat. Two minutes later, they were back on the road. He flexed his hurt leg, wishing he could take his turn behind the wheel. It wasn't right that the burden should fall entirely on Etta.

"It won't be long before we reach the prison." Her voice broke the silence that had descended in the vehicle.

"Great," he said, craning his head to check out his appearance in the side mirror. Gone was his earlier confidence in his disguise. In its place was the realization that he looked strange and artificial, like someone pretending to be something he was not.

He was starting to wonder if this was going to work.

SIX

The prison was as intimidating as he had imagined, with its massive concrete buildings and high fences with swirling loops of barbed wire on top. Etta pulled into a parking space in the visitor lot and cast a look in Steven's direction. She appeared to be exhausted, with worry lines etched across her brow. No doubt, she was thinking the same things he was. Could they really pull this off? Would the guards actually believe that he was Matt Bickler?

And what if, after all of this—the delay in leaving town and the risk to Etta, who had now become a person of interest—Greg didn't have any additional information? Or, worse, what if he was actually guilty?

Twice during the drive to the prison, he'd considered telling Etta to turn the car around. That the risk wasn't worth it. That they should forget the visit to the prison and instead just hightail it to South Dakota. But he doubted she would agree to that. She remained convinced that her brother-in-law was innocent and that he might have answers about who was after them.

Steven pulled in a deep breath and placed his fingers on the handle of the van's front door. "Okay. Here I go."

"Steven." Etta's voice was little more than a whisper.

"Yeah?"

"Just be careful. Okay?"

He tried for his most reassuring look. "It'll be fine. You know me. I'm a master at getting out of sticky situations."

"I do know you. And I know that look. It's the same swaggering smile you'd plaster on your face seconds before you got tossed by a bull."

A ripple of pleasure pinged him. Somehow, even after all these years, Etta was still able to penetrate his usual bravado. He allowed his phony grin to slip as he placed a hand on top of Etta's fingers, which were still clutching the steering wheel.

"I got this," he said. "Really. I'll be back before you know it."

Etta gave a weak smile as he stepped out and pushed the door closed behind him.

He covered the walk toward the prison quickly as dread, anxiety and adrenaline coursed through his veins. Not for the first time, he realized that, but for the grace of God, he could have ended up spending quite a few years in a place like this. He had certainly been headed down a path of crime and delinquency when he was eighteen. But, thanks to his mama's stern warnings and constant prayers, he found his way out.

He pushed open the doors and walked toward the guard behind the counter. He fished Matt Bickler's wallet out of his pocket and handed over the license. This was the first test.

"I'm here to see Greg Sanderson."

The guard glanced down at the ID, and then up at his face. A cold, clammy feeling slithered through Steven's insides, but he forced his face to remain impassive. As the uniformed deputy rechecked the license, his confidence wavered. Why hadn't he thought of a way to contact Etta if he got caught? He clenched his fingers into a fist. Should he turn around and make up an excuse to justify a sudden departure? No. That would surely alert the guards to the fact that something wasn't right. He shifted his weight. His leg was really starting to hurt.

The guard glanced up. "New glasses?" he asked with a raised eyebrow.

"Yeah. It was time for a change."

The deputy jotted something down and then directed him toward the metal detector. Once on the other side, another set of guards reviewed his ID again before allowing him through the double security doors and escorting him into a large room with tables and chairs. Wary of the scrutiny involved in an official request for an attorney-client visit, he opted to meet with Greg as part of regular visiting hours. Most of the tables were already occupied, but there was an empty spot on the far edge of the room.

Trying to act as casual as possible, Steven surveyed the plain gray walls, the linoleum floor and the half-dozen cameras mounted to the ceiling. He drummed his fingers against the table and thought about the man he was about to see. Etta was convinced that Greg was innocent. But he'd reserve judgment about that, at least for the moment.

"Who are you?" a loud voice asked, interrupting his thoughts.

Steven looked up. Greg Sanderson was not what he'd been expecting from the curated photographs he had noticed at the house along the stairs. The man standing before him, in an orange coverall and flat slippers, looked older and stressed, as if he was carrying the weight of the world on his shoulders.

"Let's keep our voices down." Steven stood up and extended his hand. "I'm Matt Bickler, a partner of Sam Colfax. Sam's out of the office today, but he asked me to come by to discuss some new information that has come up in your case."

Did any of that make sense? Steven didn't think so. But he blew out a quick sigh of relief that Greg didn't question his claim to be Matt Bickler.

"What happened?" Greg Sanderson sat down across from him at the table.

"Well, the facts are a little hazy right now, but it appears that your sister-in-law, Henrietta Mitchell, has disappeared and taken your daughter with her to—"

"Nope. No way." Greg was shaking his head before Steven had finished his sentence. "If Etta left town with Polly, she had a good reason. Maybe she needed to return to her apartment to pick up something."

"It's a bit more complicated than that. Your home was broken into, Mr. Sanderson, and your sister-in-law was attacked."

"Wait. What?" Greg's head whipped up. "Is Polly okay?"

"We have every reason to assume so."

"What's that supposed to mean?"

"Your daughter's fine," Steven said reassuringly. "We're just trying to figure out why this happened and how it affects your case."

"Probably, it's the same reason why Lilly got killed, right? And since I'm in here, what just happened can't have anything to do with me."

"True. But who is to say that you don't have an accomplice?"

Greg's brow furrowed. "An accomplice? What are you talking about? Aren't you supposed to be on my side?" The ferocity of his anger seemed to reverberate off the walls.

Steven cast a glance around the room. A few of the other visitors were looking their way, so he lowered his voice to almost a whisper. "It doesn't matter what I think. Sam just wanted me to find out if you knew anything about the break-in."

"This is the first time I'm hearing about any of this! I'm innocent. I don't think I want to talk to you anymore." Greg pushed himself up from the table. "I'll wait until Sam is available. He's my attorney. And I know he's definitely on my side."

Steven paused for a moment and took a deep breath. He needed to remain calm and not panic. He had made it this far and gained entry to the prison. But it would still be a challenge to secure Greg's trust.

He met and held Greg's gaze. "I think you should talk to me."

"Why should I?"

"Please. Give me two minutes. There are additional details I need to share."

Greg hesitated a moment, and then sank back down onto the chair. "You have sixty seconds to convince me that it will be in my best interest to discuss my case with you, Mr. Bickler." He pointed to the clock. "And your time starts now."

Steven leaned forward in his chair. The truth was all he had left, but he wasn't certain how Greg would react to it. Still, he needed to try.

"I came in here under a false identity." He leaned in. "My real name is Steven Hunt. I'm a friend of Etta's. What I told you about the home invasion is true. She and Polly are with me now, and we're trying to find out what is going on. But we need more information."

Confusion flickered in Greg's eyes. "Why not say that up front? Why come in here, claiming to be a partner of my attorney?"

"It's complicated. Matt Bickler is one of the men involved in the incident. We don't know why, but we thought you might be able to help us in some way."

Confusion marred Greg's face. "I don't know why Bickler would be involved…and I still don't understand why *you* are involved in our family situation. Last I heard from Lilly, you were still riding in the rodeo and had nothing to do with Etta."

Steven nodded. "That's true. But when I heard Lilly had died, I came to see Etta… and stumbled into the middle of the break-in. I knew your wife, too, back in the day. I heard all the stories about how their dad left when she was born, how their mom skipped town eight years later." He twisted his mouth into a wry grin. "Lilly never liked me. I think she viewed me as a threat to her relationship with Etta."

"You're right about that. She actually prided herself on helping undermine your relationship. She used to claim you were the reason that Etta was still single. That you broke her heart."

Steven couldn't help snorting. "More like the other way around. But that's ancient history. At this point, I just need for you to trust me enough to answer a few questions. Will you take me through the events of the day of the murder?"

Greg rubbed his jaw and then leaned in closer. "Can't hurt, I guess. You've probably heard it already from Etta. I woke up as usual and got ready for work. Made a pot of coffee, talked to Lilly. I was supposed to take Polly to preschool that day to give Lilly a break. But she was complaining of a stomachache, so we decided to scrap the plan. Polly was not happy about that, let me tell you. She stomped off and went to hide, but I didn't have time to go after her. When I think about how things might have been different if..." His voice trailed off as he wiped his hand across his eyes. "She used to be such a happy kid. And now she's so silent and closed off."

Steven could feel his own chest tighten in response to Greg's palpable grief and the pain he was feeling at being stuck in jail and separated from his daughter. "Okay. So you went to work. What happened next?"

"I came home at lunchtime and found Lilly on the couch. I checked her pulse, but she was already gone. I called for Polly, but she didn't come. I thought… I thought…" Greg closed his eyes and took a minute to compose himself. "I was afraid she had been hurt as well. Then, I called nine-one-one. The emergency responders arrived in minutes, but I could tell by their faces that they knew she was dead. Of course, there was an autopsy. The medical examiner found traces of poison in Lilly's coffee. And in the pot that I had admitted to making that morning. And just like that, I became suspect number one."

"It was a logical deduction."

Greg's eyes flashed as he pushed away. "Etta knows I didn't kill Lilly. But you seem to be taking the side of the police."

Steven shook his head. "Cool your jets, man. I may not be a lawyer, but I'm pretty sure the questions are going to get a lot more heated at trial. And at this point, it doesn't matter what Etta thinks about your guilt or innocence. I'm just laying out the facts."

Greg slumped back in his seat.

"You say that you didn't notice anything unusual in the weeks leading up to the murder?" Steven asked.

"Nothing that set off warning bells. But Lilly was acting different."

"Different, how?"

"It's hard to explain. She just seemed more self-pleased, like she had a secret that she didn't want to share." Greg shot him a look. "She sometimes got like that when she had some sort of big scoop involving her job at the paper. Given the normal goings-on in Silver Creek, that usually meant one of the council members was planning to resign or, most recently, some sort of scandal involving special treatment of the mayor's son. But this seemed bigger and more consuming. When I pressed her to explain, all she would say was that she was working on something big. I knew that she had consulted with an old friend of hers from juvie, a PI named Jordan Shapiro who lived in Sulphur Springs. But that's about it."

"Jordan Shapiro." Steven repeated the name to himself, committing it to memory. "Had you heard the name before?"

"No. Lilly didn't talk much about people she knew from that time in her life."

"You told the police all this?"

Greg blew out a sharp breath through his nose. "Of course. But they didn't seem interested. They had made up their minds I was guilty right off the bat, especially after they interviewed one of the neighbors who said that Lilly and I argued a lot about our finances. But it was never anything serious. We were both pretty strong-willed, so it tended to get heated when we disagreed. But once the cops heard about that, it was case closed. In their minds, Lilly's murder was just another deadly domestic dispute."

"You had money issues in your marriage?" Steven pressed.

Greg shrugged. "Who doesn't, right? But we were doing okay. Even though Lilly had always been fascinated with all sorts of get-rich-quick schemes, she was a stickler about justice. I think it had something to do with the time she spent in juvie. She really believed that no one was truly above the law. After she was killed, I searched through her things, hoping to find some clue about what she was up to. I hit a dead end on that, so I thought about asking around the neighborhood and got a recommendation for a good lawyer."

"Right. Sam Colfax. What did you hear about him?"

Greg smirked. "You mean your pseudo partner? What do you want to know?"

Before Steven could answer, the guard

tapped him on the shoulder and pointed at the clock. His time was up.

"Maybe we can talk later. But one last thing before I go." Steven lowered his voice to a whisper. "It would probably be best if you didn't say anything about my visit. It might come out eventually, but as far as you know, the only person you spoke to today was an attorney from your law firm."

Greg made a motion of sealing his lips as Steven stood up and walked toward the door. Was it his imagination, or was one of the guards following his movements with his eyes? Maybe it was all part of the job. Still, the faster he got back into the car, the better. There had been a couple of dicey moments, but his meeting with Greg had proven to be worth the risk.

Etta adjusted her position in the driver's seat and, for the fifth time in as many minutes, peered out the window at the near-empty parking lot next to the prison. What was taking Steven so long? At this point, she was fairly certain that he'd made it inside. But then what? She could easily imagine Greg making a fuss and refusing to answer any questions.

And what if a vigilant guard had allowed Steven to enter but then called the law office to double-check his identity? The police could at this very moment be on their way to arrest Steven for impersonating a member of the bar.

Was that even a crime? She wasn't sure, but she could not allow herself to think that way. *Focus on the positive.* She closed her eyes and tried to imagine the best-case scenario. But her moment of peace and quiet was interrupted by a man in a tan uniform knocking on the driver's side door.

Uh-oh. Had he somehow recognized her from the picture that had been on TV? She pulled down her ball cap and rolled down the window.

The man's thin gray hair fluffed up in wisps along his sunburned scalp as he held up a laminated state ID. "I noticed some movement inside the van, so I thought I'd come over and make sure everything's under control."

Etta took a deep breath, relief roiling though her senses. So far, anyway, he didn't seem to have connected her with what had happened in Silver Creek. She just needed to stay calm and not act suspicious. And to stick to the truth as much as possible.

"Everything is fine, sir. My niece and I are waiting for a friend who's inside visiting an inmate. Is that okay?"

"No worries. We keep tabs on all vehicles parked in the lot, but when I ran your plates, I saw that you were driving a rental. Not that there's any problem with that. I just wanted to check things out and make sure you were okay."

Etta waited until the man had moved on to the other side of the lot before turning to check on Polly. Poor kid. Etta could only hope that Polly hadn't fully comprehended most of the events of the past few days. "Do you want anything to eat or drink?" she asked.

Polly stared back. A slight shake of the head was the only sign that that her words had registered.

Etta fought the desire to sigh. Showing exasperation wouldn't help Polly feel more comfortable. "Do you want to play 'I spy'?" she said, trying again.

Another minuscule shake of the head from Polly.

Well, that was probably just as well since there wasn't much to see in the prison parking lot. Etta scanned the area. What would it be like to be confined within these walls for years at a time? A shiver ran up her spine. Maybe now, she'd find out sooner rather than later.

She had been so adamant about not involving the authorities when she had first been attacked. Was it really only yesterday that she had killed that man in self-defense? She shook her head. It seemed like weeks. Maybe Steven was right. Maybe it would have been better to call 911. She hadn't done anything wrong. But she knew only too well that law enforcement didn't just mean the police. It also included social services. And there was no way she was going to let anyone take Polly away from her.

A rustle from the back seat reclaimed her attention. She swiveled her head to see Polly, clutching her stuffed rabbit.

"I like your bunny. Does she have a name?"

Polly blinked back.

A knot of sorrow tightened in Etta's chest. Not for the first time, she regretted letting time slip by without visiting Lilly and Greg. If only Polly trusted her a bit more. Maybe talking about Lilly would lessen Polly's wariness.

"Did you know that your mom and I had a pet growing up?"

A flicker of interest seemed to glint in Polly's eyes.

"Yes," Etta continued. "Except it wasn't a rabbit. It was a dog. And it wasn't really our pet. She was a stray who lived in the neighborhood. Your mom named her Jane. I tried to tell her that wasn't a proper name for a dog, but she didn't care."

Polly blinked. She seemed to be waiting for more.

"Actually, Jane saved my life. Jane and your mom." Etta paused. For years, she hadn't allowed herself to dwell on memories from her childhood. Everyone, including Lilly, had advised her that denial wasn't healthy, but so far it had been working just fine for her. Well, one story wouldn't hurt. Not if it gained her some trust with Polly.

"Jane was quite a silly dog. She used to wander through the streets sniffing for food. But if someone tried to feed her something, she would back away. Oh, and she never barked. When she saw your mom, her tail would wag, and she'd trot over to be petted.

"Well, one Thanksgiving, when I was about thirteen, I'd been sent to the grocery store to buy dinner." She could well remember how much she'd dreaded waiting in line and having to pay with food stamps. Of course, they tried to make it less embarrassing with the prepaid cards, but she knew that the checker knew what it meant. That she was poor. That her mama couldn't hold down a job. Not that the grubby jeans that were two sizes two small and hit above the ankle weren't a give-away. Or the sneaker with a hole at the toe. But buying groceries was somehow the worst. A new level of humiliation.

"Anyway, on this particular afternoon, I'd saved up some of my own money from weeding our neighbor's garden and bought a turkey. A real, frozen turkey." Again, the memory wrapped itself around her. Her pride in making the purchase with her own money. They hadn't had a real Thanksgiving din-ner for a few years, and she'd had all sorts of lofty dreams of cooking it for hours and then serving it to her family for dinner. Why she'd thought that she would be able to cook a tur-key without any experience was still beyond her, but, at thirteen years old, she hadn't been quite as worried about the details.

Too bad those good feelings hadn't lasted.

The touch of a hand on her arm called her back to the present. Polly had reached out to her. Etta stared down at the tiny fingers and fought back the desire to cry. She and her sister had spent most of their childhood confused and lonely. And now the cycle seemed to be continuing for Polly. It wasn't fair.

But, obviously, Polly was expecting some sort of happy ending to the story. Etta tamped down her feelings. She needed to keep it light and not scare Polly more than she already was.

"Well, a turkey is cold and heavy, and I had to walk home. It wasn't far. About a mile and half. But by the time I had gone just a few blocks, my arms were getting tired. A part of me wanted to just give up and leave the turkey in the street and go home. But I had been so excited, so I kept trudging on. Well, I must not have been paying attention, because all of a sudden, I stubbed my toe on the sidewalk. The turkey slipped from my fingers and landed on my foot, and then I fell down. It was like a chain reaction of unfortunate events. Bing, bang. Boom."

Etta willed her voice to make the event sound funny and was rewarded when a ghost of smile wavered on Polly's face.

"But when I tried to get up, my foot hurt too much to walk. So I just had to sit down by the side of the road. A couple of people drove past and offered to help, but I said no. I just sat there and waited. And waited. And waited. And then, guess who came by? Jane. She walked right up to me and let me scratch her ears. It was starting to get dark, so I was a little scared. Jane sat right next to me, and I put my arm around her neck and really wanted to cry. But after a little while, she stood up and walked away, too. And then I was really lonely." She smiled down at Polly.

"Meanwhile, your mom was at home waiting. She knew that I usually brought her a couple of lollipops when I went to the store, so she was on the lookout for my return. Well, I didn't know this at the time, but Jane didn't actually abandon me on the side of the road. She went to find your mom. Lilly told me later that Jane trotted up, but instead of greeting her with a handshake, she pawed the ground. When Lilly saw that, she knew something was wrong, and she went to get help from one of our neighbors."

A movement from outside the van caused her eyes to dart toward the window, and a wild fluttering of relief and joy erupted in her chest. There was Steven, strolling back toward the car, as relaxed as someone out for a walk in the park. She turned back toward Polly. Time to wrap up her story. Steven didn't need to hear any more details about her dysfunctional childhood. Not when his own had been so picture-perfect.

Probably best not to describe what had really happened next, how she and Lilly had eaten cereal for Thanksgiving dinner, and a cold towel had been wrapped around Etta's swollen foot. Polly needed a happy ending. So did she, for that matter. She forced her lips to curve upward. Except that it actually didn't seem fake. Her mouth wanted to smile.

"Well, the neighbor found me and gave me a ride home. And there was your mom and Jane waiting for me. Together they had saved me. Can you imagine? My baby sister and a dog that wouldn't bark were able to get help."

Polly pulled her rabbit closer to her chest and gave a little sigh. For once, it didn't sound like a sigh of worry or anxiety, but one of contentment.

A second later, Steven pulled open the van door and climbed into the passenger seat. He gave a discreet thumbs-up to Etta and then turned to smile at Polly.

"How did it go?" Etta asked.

"Better than expected," Steven said. "How did you do with Polly?"

Etta shrugged. "Okay, I guess. I was worried that they would see through your disguise, so I got really nervous when a guard came by and knocked on the window. But he was just interested in the van because he had run the plates and saw that it was a rental. When I explained that I was waiting for someone, he left."

Steven let out a long sigh. "This is not good, Etta."

"But he didn't recognize me. And he didn't ask who I was waiting for."

Steven shook his head. "Maybe we're okay for the moment. But we can't take the chance that he won't eventually make the connection."

SEVEN

Etta was sitting ramrod-straight as she clutched the wheel, her eyes fixed forward. To say she looked tense would be an understatement.

What happened at the prison was his fault, not hers. He shouldn't have asked her to wait for him in the lot. But what was done was done. Their options were becoming more and more limited. He needed to think outside the box.

Inspiration struck as he remembered a text from his buddy who was riding this week at a county fair in Leesburg, which was only about an hour or so away. Donny was a good guy, and it didn't take much convincing to talk him into a temporary swap of his Airstream camper for the rented van. In theory. It seemed like a perfect solution. Once they made the switch, they would once again be off the radar. They could head north without any worries about stopping and being recognized at restaurants or motels.

"Don't worry, Etta." He reached over and touched her hand. "This is a good plan."

"I don't know, Steven. It seems like everything we do is one step forward, two steps back. I just hope there was something positive that came out of your visit with Greg."

"There was. Definitely. Your brother-in-law did share some interesting information about Lilly. Are you familiar with the name Jordan Shapiro?"

Her forehead creased. "No."

"Well, apparently, she's a PI friend of your sister, living in Sulphur Springs. Lilly reached out to her for advice about something she was working on. Said it could blow up into something big."

"What was it about?"

He shrugged. "Greg didn't know."

"Sounds like we need to talk to this Jordan Shapiro and get more information."

Steven shook his head. "Uh-uh. Remember? You agreed that we would drive straight to South Dakota once we found out what Greg had to say."

"I know I did." She glanced his way. "But

now that we know about this, we can't leave Texas without checking it out."

"Sure we can." They couldn't stay here—the men following them would catch up soon enough. And the sooner he got home, the sooner he could get Seb's help with this mess. "When we get to the ranch, you can call Lilly's friend and find out what she has to say."

"She might not talk to me on the phone, Steven. Our best hope would be for me to make a personal appeal as Lilly's sister. Besides, Sulphur Springs isn't far off the route to South Dakota. In any case, it can be a quick stop. Not much more than an hour delay."

An hour delay? Not likely. And right now, his main concern was making it to Leesburg without being pulled over by the police. He could tell Etta understood the risks as she kept the speed at a steady two miles over the limit.

Truth to tell, this was not the way he had planned to spend his six-month recuperation. He remembered the wary smile on the doctor's face as she signed his release forms from the hospital. "You'll be fine," she had said. "As long as you take it easy. No vigorous exercise or undue stress. Grab a stack of good books, and settle back and relax. Better yet,

do your reading on a deck chair under an um-
brella on a warm beach." Toes in the water...
Now that sounded good.

Well, Texas was warm. Or, warmish. But
getting knocked around in a fight with a thug
with at least thirty pounds on him wasn't exactly what the doctor had ordered. He'd realized that the moment the first punch was
thrown at Lilly and Greg's house in Silver
Creek. So why had he stuck around?

Once again, he shifted his eyes toward the
driver's side of the car, hoping to check out
Etta's current mood. Hmm. Hard to say. She
was frowning as she peered at a cluster of
signs ahead.

"Our turn isn't for a dozen or so miles,"
he said.

"Thanks," she answered without turning
her head. He had never been an expert when
it came to women, but was it possible she was
annoyed at him? Why? Unless, of course, she
could read his mind and sense his regret.

His mood was less regretful and more circumspect. Wary of risks.

Bottom line, he had decided to come to
Texas on a whim. Hop a bus south and see
the country from the inside of a Greyhound.
Spend some time thinking about life and

love and his next thirty years. Yeah, he had wanted to see Etta, but with no illusions that their eyes would meet and the years would fall away. He was smart enough to know that what had happened between them was part of a past that could not be reclaimed.

"Steven?" Etta turned suddenly to face him. "Can we take another minute to review the plan?"

Not mad, then. Just anxious. He could deal with that.

"Sure." He checked the time on his phone. "We'll be in Leesburg within the hour. The fairgrounds are on the north side of town, and Donny's Airstream will be parked in the area adjacent to the main lot. He flies a POW/MIA flag, so the trailer should be easy to spot. The key's under the mat, and he said we should go in and make ourselves comfortable. I'll head off to visit with Donny, and you can color your hair. As soon as I get back, we can hit the road."

She gripped the wheel. "But what about our visit to Jordan Shapiro?"

Frustration bit at his senses. He had given in to Etta every step along the way. His suggestion that she turn herself in to the police had been met first with stonewalling and then an outright refusal to even consider the option. And while the decision to seek shelter at the ranch had been made, the drive north kept getting rerouted and delayed.

"I don't think so. Etta. It's getting too dangerous for us to stay any longer in Texas."

She shook her head. "Fine. We can talk about it later. Look!" She pointed to a sign up ahead that showed the exit to Leesburg. "We're almost there."

Once they were off the main road, it was just a short drive to the fairgrounds and a cluster of caravans and tents that formed a small city to the left of the main lot. Etta honed right in on the distinctive black-and-white flag flying next to the front door.

"Does your friend Donny know someone who was a prisoner of war?"

Steven nodded. "His dad was in Vietnam. Some of his friends went missing and never came home."

"Flying the flag is a good way to keep their memory alive."

The Airstream looked smaller than Steven remembered, but the keys were right where his buddy had left them. He had a moment of trepidation as he pushed open the door. But inside, the tiny home was compact and tidy.

Two adults and a child in such a small space would be tight, to be sure, but it would do just fine. Besides, beggars couldn't be choosers. Steven smiled as he recalled his mom's favorite words of wisdom for him and his brother.

Etta paused on the threshold as she spotted a black-and-yellow gun on a shelf next to the door. "Is that what I think it is?"

Steven stepped forward to check it out. "A Taser? Yeah. Donny must have bought it to deal with vandals who sometimes roam around these kinds of fairs. I'll put it in the glove compartment and lock it up. That way we won't need to worry about Polly getting hurt."

"Good idea… If we take the Airstream, where will your buddy sleep? Isn't this where he's been living?"

Steven shrugged. "He'll bunk in with one of the other riders. Most of the guys travel in campers, so there's always room for a friend in need. Speaking of which, I better change my clothes and head over to the fairgrounds to meet Donny." He reached out and grabbed one of three cowboy hats that were hanging next to the door. "I was wondering what happened to this. Must have left it here last time I stayed with Donny." He pulled the brim low on his head. "I'll probably be gone for about an hour or so. Will you guys be okay?"

Etta nodded. "I think so. I'll bring in the groceries and make Polly something to eat. Then, maybe I'll take a shot at coloring my hair. It just feels odd to be poking around in someone else's home."

"If you knew Donny, you'd realize he's happy to help. Here. Take these just in case." He handed her a set of keys and watched as she slipped them into the pocket of her pants. "It would probably be best not to wander outside. It's just a guess, but I assume that a more up-to-date picture of you is now being shown on the news. Best to keep a low profile and stay inside the Airstream."

Etta stared at the description on the box of hair dye that Steven had purchased at the mini-mart along the road. Intense dark red. "Ugh," she said out loud, shaking her head. Polly sidled up next to her, anxious for a peek. "What do you think, Polls? Maybe a bit too flashy for your stodgy aunt?"

A wisp of a smile creased Polly's lips.

"I agree. I'm not sure why Steven thinks I can pull off being a redhead."

She spread out the instructions and began

to read. It looked complicated, especially the part about sectioning the hair and clipping it out of the way on the top of her head. "Maybe I should do the cutting part first. That way, I won't run out of dye."

Polly picked a picture book from the pile Etta had hauled in from the car and settled down on the floor to read.

The Airstream, though compact, was as fully functional as any of the places she found herself living on the job as a traveling nurse. There was a tiny kitchen with a two-burner stove, a sink, a refrigerator and even a small microwave tucked under the counter. Two small couches could quickly be converted into pullout beds, and under the windows was a folding kitchen table. The place was fully air-conditioned; though today, with the temperature outside hovering in the sixties, a bank of open windows next to the door provided a refreshing breeze. "I could be very happy living in a place like this," Etta said as she headed into the tiny bathroom, scissors in hand.

This was going to be difficult, but it needed to be done. Her long, flowing hair had been a part of her for so long. On the job, she often wore it pulled back in a French braid, or, if she was pressed for time, a simple ponytail. But this was not the moment to be sentimental about an old hairstyle. A new color and cut were the quickest way to change her appearance.

Fifteen minutes later, the bathroom trash can was filled with strands of long dark hair. Etta frowned at her reflection in the mirror. A short new style. Not bad, but not all that good, either. Back in the day, she remembered someone calling that particular cut a "pixie," and she had to admit that there was something elflike about her new look.

She took one last glance in the mirror and reached for the instruction sheet for the dye. It seemed simple enough. Mix the tube of applicator cream with the developer and then use the brush to paint it on the hair. A pungent, ammonia-like scent assailed her nostrils as she worked methodically to cover each section with clumpy, grayish dye. When she finished, she slipped on the clear plastic shower cap that came with the kit and looked at the clock. Well, she had gone and done it. In thirty-five minutes, she'd be a redhead.

With nothing else to do, she wandered out to the main living area and sat down next to Polly, watching the little girl as she carefully turned the pages of her picture books. It was a strangely relaxing activity, and she found herself drifting off to sleep. She awoke with a start to see that she had only a few minutes to go before the final step in the coloring process. She was on her way to the bathroom to rinse off the solution when high-pitched cries from outside in the campground stopped her in her tracks. What was going on? The view out of the front window was split by a stand of dusty evergreens, but the body of a young boy crumpled on the ground could be seen clearly a dozen yards down the dirt road. Two women stood beside the child, pacing and shouting.

"We need a doctor! Now!"

Etta sprang into action. She wrapped one of Donny's red, white and blue scarves around her head. Steven's reminder that she shouldn't leave the Airstream flitted through her mind, but how could she ignore a cry for assistance? It would only take a few minutes to assess the situation and call 911. Besides, no one would recognize her with a scarf tied over her hair.

"Wait here, Polly. I'll be right back," she called out as she slipped into the late afternoon shadows of the campground. A crowd had already gathered around the body of the small child. The boy was moaning, a good sign since it meant he was conscious. But her relief turned into concern as she saw the blood pooling next to the arm that he was clutching to his chest. A pair of hedge-trimming sheers, with telltale blood spatter, was lying inches away in the dirt. An accident, then. But had the sharp blades hit an artery, and if so, should she apply an emergency tourniquet to staunch the flow?

"I'm a nurse," she said as she kneeled down beside the child and applied direct pressure to the wound. "Did someone call for an ambulance?"

"We dialed nine-one-one, but no one answered," one of the women claimed.

"Keep calling, Joann," an authoritative voice urged. "They have to be there."

"It hurts!" the little boy wailed, and Etta's adrenaline kicked into overdrive.

"I need a piece of thin cloth to make a tourniquet," she said. Someone tossed her a white T-shirt, and she twisted it into a triangular band, which she wrapped around the little boy's arm. "Can one of you find a stick? Or a pencil or a spoon? Something that will allow me to increase the pressure and stop the bleeding."

Someone in the crowd handed her a metal spoon. It was small but sturdy, and it would do as a windlass for the tourniquet. Etta tied off the ends of the cloth and inserted the spoon as she prepared for tightening. She leaned in closer to reassure her patient. "This might hurt a little," she whispered softly. The kid stared back at her with worried eyes.

A loud commotion caused the crowd to part, and a short woman in a colorful dress appeared beside her. "I'm Ricky's mom," she said, her voice shaking. She glanced at her son. "Hang in there, hon. This lady is going to help you until the ambulance gets here. Just squeeze my hand if the pain gets too strong."

The little boy nodded, his wide eyes full of tears.

Etta knew from experience how the increased tension of the tourniquet often caused a patient to cry out from the discomfort, but Ricky seemed brave. The 911 call must have finally been answered because soon the sound of a siren split the air, the wail growing louder and louder as a small fire truck and an ambulance blew up clouds of dust on the road.

Moments later, a team of paramedics arrived on the scene. "We'll take it from here.

But that sure is a nice tourniquet, lady," one of the EMTs said.

"You got it on there real good," the taller of the two added as Etta scrambled to her feet, yielding her place to the professionals.

Gaze firmly fixed on the ground, she took one step back and then another, slowly fading into the background as the firefighters made a first attempt at crowd control.

Well, that was that, then. It was reassuring to see the flashing lights of the rescue vehicles and to hear the squeaking of the wheels of the gurney as it was pulled across the dry dirt road. She had done her best to help, and she hadn't been recognized. No one had stopped her to ask any questions about who she was and what she was doing here. All eyes were glued to the brave little boy still holding his mom's hand.

Etta retreated toward the Airstream, and, with one final glance to make sure no one was watching, ducked inside. Overwhelmed with exhaustion and relief, she leaned against the wall and pulled in a long breath. Polly's gaze met hers in a tacit sort of understanding. If her niece could speak, Etta imagined her saying, *Glad you're back. Now tell me what happened.*

She needed to remove the headscarf and rinse the now-tacky color solution out of her hair. With wet hair, it was too soon to reveal the consequences of the fifteen-minute delay. There was nothing she could do about it, so she returned to Polly's side and began to describe the brave little boy who had accidentally cut his arm and the triumphant arrival of the first responders.

Suddenly Etta had a sensation that the pockets of her pants felt just a bit lighter than they had earlier, and she realized that she had dropped the keys to the Airstream. She remembered bending down to apply the tourniquet and feeling something slide out of her pocket and onto the dirt. She peeked again out the window. The crowd appeared to be breaking up as the paramedics loaded the boy into the ambulance.

So what to do about retrieving the keys? She had avoided detection the first time around. Could she do it again? She could wait until Steven returned and ask him to help search, but she was still hoping they could leave as soon as he got back from visiting with his friend.

Maybe she was overthinking this. The keys were probably still in the exact spot where she had kneeled down to assist the little boy. But just in case they weren't, she'd take Polly along to help with the search.

With the shrill scream of a siren, the ambulance and the fire truck departed and the crowd dispersed. Now that the excitement was over, there was nothing more to see.

"Hey, Polly. I seem to have dropped my keys outside. Will you come along and help me look for them?"

Polly stood up, and Etta reached for her ball cap and tightened it so it fit her little niece's head.

As they made their way toward the site of the accident, Etta swept her gaze across the flattened patch of new grass and fresh tire tracks, past the crimson stain of blood pooled on the ground, and the rusty hedge trimmers still lying half-open in the dirt.

But there was no sign of the keys.

"Someone probably picked them up," Etta mused. "Maybe a neighbor..." She lifted her eyes toward the front of a nearby trailer. The curtains twitched.

A youngish man with a scraggly goatee answered on the first knock.

"I just got home from work," he barked gruffly once she explained the reason for the interruption. "But I heard about the commotion from my wife. And now that I think about it, she may have mentioned something about finding some keys. Said she had an idea who might have dropped them, but she thought it would be best to turn them in at the lost and found at the grandstand."

EIGHT

There was something strangely comforting about the dusty paths lined with fairy lights, the pop-up vendors selling fried food and the throngs of people swarming around the grandstand. It had been more than a decade since Etta's last trip to a county fair. But the sounds and smells that permeated the air reminded her of the evening she'd first met Steven.

Then again, maybe *met* wasn't the right word to describe that first encounter. She had been twenty-one back then, out for a day of fun with a group of fellow nurses from the hospital. Her mood had been relaxed and nearly carefree, though as guardian of a sulky teenager, she hadn't had the luxury of ever being completely free of worries. But it was definitely one of the less stressful times in her life. It had been purely happenstance that they had stopped to watch a bull-riding competition. A fluke that she had gone down to buy peanuts at a stand near the ring when a cowboy climbed onto the back of a bull named Midnight Mansion, only to be bucked off the enormous animal's back and then trampled into the dirt.

She shivered to imagine how much worse it would have been if Steven hadn't been wearing a helmet, a face mask and a protective vest. Even so, the spectacle in the ring had caused the crowd to gasp in horror as a trio of cowboys worked to distract the bull so the medic on call could attend to Steven.

It was horrible, even worse from Etta's close-up perspective. She recalled the anxious hush, followed by high-pitched shouting as the gates were pushed wide for a small ambulance.

Etta had pushed forward into the ring, certain she could help in some small way. Even now, as she replayed the scene in her head, she wondered why she had been allowed to pass through the gates. But there she'd been, kneeling next to the staff doctor, offering a weak smile as Steven's eyes blinked open and then closed as he winced with pain. And then, as the rest of the medical team arrived, she had taken a step back, quickly consigned to the role of spectator. That moment in the ring would forever remain seared in her memory.

Now, as she approached the grandstand, it was the scent of those roasting peanuts that still made her mouth water after all these years.

Would it be foolish to stop at one of the vendors to purchase a few snacks for herself and Polly? With her short choppy red hair tickling the back of her ears, she felt like a new person, but she resisted the temptation to stop as she trudged forward, searching for a sign that would lead her to the lost and found.

"What do you think, Polly? Do you like the fair?"

The little girl replied by wrinkling her nose.

Etta laughed. "Yeah. It does have a different smell. But you get used to it. Steven used to say this is real life. And that the city is what smells wrong."

She could picture him wrinkling his nose just like Polly when she would sit with him in the hospital, his dark hair rumpled and his lips quirked in his trademark half smile. He'd claimed to hate being confined to a bed, explaining that the air was too clean, too artificial, too plain. That he belonged in the country, riding a horse, or better yet, hanging on for dear life on the back of a bucking bull.

Well, look where that had gotten him, she'd been tempted to say. But she'd offered no criticism. How could she—her heart was already melting at the sight of those teasing dark eyes.

Yeah, those had been the days. More good than bad in a lot of ways. For years, she hadn't allowed herself to dwell on the past, to recall stories from her childhood or to relive that whirlwind romance. Lilly used to say that Etta played things close to the vest. Even at her sister's funeral, when friends and neighbors had gathered to celebrate her life, Etta hadn't offered up any old memories of the bond they had shared, always as sisters and sometimes as friends. Yet somehow, spending time with Steven, it was as if the lid she had kept so carefully locked on her past had suddenly been blown off, and it all came flooding back in a torrent.

She shook her head and tightened her grip on Polly's fingers for a moment. This is exactly what she didn't need. It was time to face some cold, hard facts. Lilly was dead. And Steven hadn't sought her out intending to rekindle their past relationship. Instead, he'd been hijacked into helping them by the circumstances of his arrival. He was kind. She had always known that. And it was his kindness that had caused him to get involved in her problems, just as it had been his kindness that had instigated his proposal all those years ago. Oh, sure, he had claimed to be in love with her, but he had also fancied himself her knight in shining armor, rescuing the girl from the wrong side of the tracks and offering her a better life. She hadn't wanted that then, and she didn't want it now.

She and Polly needed him right now, she'd admit that. But she couldn't allow herself to dwell on a misty dream of what could have been. Steven was still the same overly confident, cocky bull rider, and she was the same independent-minded nurse who was determined to have her own career.

A tug on her arm brought her back to the present, and she realized she was squeezing Polly's hand.

"Sorry, Pol." She relaxed her fingers, looking down at the little girl. "Do you think you can be my helper? We're looking for a table or a stall with a sign that says 'Lost and Found.'"

Polly stared up at her, blank-faced. Right. Polly's reading skills were limited at best.

But the kid was smart, she'd give her that. The way she put her fingers over the words in her books. Almost as if she was trying to pull them off the page and keep them for herself.

If only Polly would talk… Etta couldn't begin to imagine what she would say. The little girl's face—alternately happy, sad, lonely and content—had been Etta's only window to what was going on inside her head. And right now, her niece's expression revealed deep dismay. Etta stifled the sigh welling up in her chest. It was the same old story. One step forward, two steps back. That was what her interactions with Polly felt like. Every time there was the hint of a breakthrough, something would happen that would cause her niece to pull inward again.

And just like that, her excitement at exploring the fairgrounds dimmed. Who was she kidding? She was completely out of her element here. It was as if all the stress and exhaustion from the last two days had suddenly thrown a heavy mantle around her shoulders, physically pulling her down. She needed to find the keys and return to the Airstream. Steven was probably already back there, wondering where they had gone.

"Excuse me, sir," she said to an official-looking man in khaki shorts and a white shirt. "Can you point me in the direction of the lost and found?"

"You just passed it," he said, pointing toward a building behind them. "It's in a little booth to the right of the entry door. You can't miss it."

Etta muttered a quick thanks, then turned to retrace her steps. "C'mon, Polly!" She injected some forced pep into her voice. "We're almost there."

As they stepped back inside the open barn, her nostrils were once again assailed by the scent of animals and hay as she led Polly past cows of all shapes and sizes awaiting a best-of-breed competition. The signs on the front of the stalls identified them as Holsteins, Angus, Shorthorn and Longhorn. And from the size of the crowds milling around, there seemed to be much interest in comparing the unique characteristics as well as the size and coloring of each breed. Following the official's directions, Etta headed to the right. There, just as the man had said, was a little booth claiming to be the lost and found. Etta quickened her steps, pulling Polly along with her.

"Can I help you with something?" a dark-haired woman behind the counter asked.

Etta nodded. "I lost my keys at the campground, and someone suggested they might be here."

"Oh, of course. Are you the lady who helped little Ricky?" The woman's eyes were fixed downward as she rummaged through a drawer. "We heard all about his accident and how you arrived out of nowhere and knew just what to do. Actually, dear, Ricky's uncle stopped by. His parents are at the hospital. But he asked me to thank you for saving his nephew's life."

Etta smiled. "I just did what anyone would do."

"Hmm," the woman murmured, still looking through the drawer. "I'm not finding any keys in here. Now, where did I put them? Oh, I know! I stuck them in the jar with the lost lighters." She turned toward a cabinet on the back wall but kept up her steady stream of chitchat. "Well, it was certainly providential that you were able to help. From what I heard, you really saved the day. I told Carl, that's the uncle, you can't be too careful. Kids can get hurt in the strangest ways. My neighbor's son almost died when he was run over by his riding lawn mower. And don't even get me started about all the crazy people in the city.

Carjackings and assaults. I'm just grateful to live in the country. Oh, here they are!"

The woman swung back around as Etta stretched her hand over the counter, eager to claim the keys the woman held in her hand.

"Now, what was I going on about? Oh, right, can't be too careful these days. Why, did you see that story about the little girl who went missing in that town outside Dallas?"

An icy shiver ran up Etta's spine. "I must have missed that one." She made a show of looking down at her watch. "But, oh, I'm sorry. I've got to run. I'm meeting a friend at the grandstand."

The lost-and-found lady was staring now, her eyes fixed squarely on Polly. The silence stretched for only a few seconds, but for Etta, it felt like she had fallen into a void of growing dread as the woman set the keys out of reach on the back counter and pushed a form in front of her instead.

"Actually, you need to sign this before I hand over your property. We keep a record of all transactions. That way we don't have people trying to claim something that isn't theirs."

She could tell that the woman was stalling, and she realized with a start that Polly had removed the ball cap covering her hair, making her instantly recognizable as the missing child in that Amber Alert.

Etta shifted back on her heels. The quicker she and Polly got out of here, the better.

The lost-and-found woman excused herself, scooting around the counter as she hurried toward one of the khaki-clad officials standing by the door. The man took out his walkie-talkie, his glance shifting slyly toward Polly.

Etta had seen enough. Just then, a large group shuffled past the area, and she reached over the counter and snatched back her keys. After lifting Polly into her arms, she jogged toward the exit.

Khaki-clad officials appeared to be everywhere. She could spot four without even turning her head. And they all seemed to have their ears glued to their walkie-talkies.

"Some people are looking for us, Polly," she said as she edged closer to the exit of the building. "But we don't want them to find us because we've planned an adventure. We're going to hide for a while and then go back to the Airstream, okay?"

Polly's head slowly bobbed up and down.

Etta stepped quickly through the door. A worn path led to another barn with a sign that claimed it was closed to the public. Perfect. She quickly ducked inside. Rows of small stalls lined the back wall, and Etta headed for one in the farthest corner, where a half-dozen bales of hay were stacked in a pile. "Good cover for hiding," she whispered to Polly as she sank to the ground and settled the little girl on her lap. Tucking her knees up, Etta lowered her head, trying to make herself as small as possible. She squeezed her eyes closed for half of a second, and then forced them open, letting out a squeak of surprise as she stared into the beady eyes of a scraggly goat. "He—or she—seems friendly," she said. The goat held her gaze, trying to size up the unexpected intrusion.

With all the bleating and chomping and rustling of hay, it was hard to hear what was happening outside their little stall. As the minutes passed, she entertained herself by imagining that no one was looking for them, that she had overreacted, that the woman at the lost and found hadn't recognized her, after all. A bubble of relief began to grow in her chest as she allowed herself to dwell on that pleasant possibility. She stroked Polly's hair and waited. The little girl was getting impatient as seconds turned to minutes, and then minutes to almost an hour. She stretched out her foot and kicked the hay into a pile. Etta checked her watch. If another fifteen minutes passed without any signs of activity nearby, it ought to be safe to move on.

"Hey!" A voice broke through the noises around her. "Did you see a woman with a little girl?" The beam of a flashlight made a long pass through the barn's interior, stopping for a moment in the stall to the right.

Etta froze. The voice was strangely familiar. She had definitely heard it before, but she wasn't sure where.

"Nah, we didn't see anyone," someone responded even as the yellow circle of light passed inches from the spot where Etta and Polly were hiding. "We closed up early today. Not too many people are interested in goats, you know. The horses and the pigs are the popular spots." There was a long pause. "What's going on? Are you with the police?"

"What do you think?" was the gruff reply. "Why else would I be mucking around in a goat barn? This is serious business, bucko. This woman is known to be armed and dangerous. She killed a cop and kidnapped a kid. So you better watch your back and take some care."

Killed a cop? No. That wasn't true. The man who assaulted her had broken into her home, attacked her and Steven. Clearly, *he* was the criminal—bent on kidnapping Polly.

Etta waited a few minutes longer and then snuck a peek over the hay. The gruff-voiced man appeared to be gone, and in his place was a woman wearing a straw hat and carrying a baby goat. An older man with a shaggy moustache followed behind her, lugging a large crate.

"What did that guy want?" the woman asked her companion.

"Information about some lady and kid. Claimed to be a cop, but he sure didn't look like one with that wild gray beard and those crazy eyes. In any case, this sounds like trouble. Last time something like this happened, they shut down all the exits to the fair."

Where were Etta and Polly? Not inside the Airstream, that was for sure. Steven had figured that out in a matter of seconds. But it was hard to believe they would have gone far.

It was too soon to panic. At least not yet. He was tempted to ask a few of the neighbors if they had seen a woman and a little girl. But he'd rather not say too much—not unless he had to. And, at the moment, he was tired and anxious and slightly on edge. It had been great to see Donny, but he had felt vaguely uncomfortable reliving the glory days when they were major competitors in the ring. It seemed that he no longer had the heart for it.

It had taken a long time to understand, but eventually it had dawned on him that, while he loved riding bulls and he enjoyed the camaraderie of his fellow riders, he no longer relished the notoriety that came with winning championships. His first love had been for the adrenaline rush he experienced whenever he'd strapped onto a bull. But the more time he spent on the circuit, the more he had come to realize that it was the bulls themselves that were his passion.

Since his vaunted comeback, he was more popular than ever. Apparently, the only thing more impressive than winning the championship was jumping into the arena to save a friend. Now he was being hailed, not as a great bull rider, but as a hero. And he felt like a fraud.

Where was Etta, anyway? Maybe if he strolled around the campsite, someone would offer him information rather than him having to seek it out. Actually, hadn't he noticed a uniformed police officer along with members of the security team strolling around the fair? A tickle of apprehension nudged him. In and of itself, it wasn't unusual for there to be guards in the area, since campers could become rowdy. But a uniformed police officer was definitely not the norm.

He began to pick his away along the road, hoping to encounter a friendly stranger who might have seen Etta and Polly.

He spotted a boy, about fourteen, walking with an older man who looked like his father. Both of them were decked out in camo-patterned overalls and sporting hats with the logo of the Professional Bull Riders circuit, PBR. "Hey, there," Steven said, trying on his best smile. "I just pulled in for the night. What's with the extra security?"

The teen smirked. "You know these rent-a-cop types. They're all a bunch of tools. Think they're going to catch a big-time criminal just because Mrs. Swallows claims she spotted a fugitive."

"Kenny…" The older man's voice had a rebuking tone. "Don't be telling tales that might not be true." He held out his hand. "Name's Carl. Carl Deering. And who are you? You don't sound like you're from Texas."

"You're right about that." Steven nodded. "I'm from South Dakota. But I used to ride the circuit."

"You don't say. Kenny here is hoping to make the cut the next couple of years. So you were asking about the police. I don't know the story, but they're wandering around asking all sorts of questions about this woman they say is a fugitive. Plainclothes and uniformed cops. Not that anyone is talking. Whoever the lady is, she saved my nephew from bleeding out. We all saw it. She's good, in our book."

Steven sighed. So that explained why Etta had disregarded her own safety—to help a hurt kid. But what happened after that?

It would be smart not to act too interested. Best to change the subject and then circle back to the stuff he wanted to know. "I get it. I saw some of the craziest stuff when I was trying to make it onto the circuit. One time, a friend of mine found a pig inside his Winnebago eating his sheets."

Carl threw back his head and laughed. "I've never heard that one before. But there sure are some good tales." His face sobered for a minute. "This was real serious, though. Ricky was bleeding all over, screaming his head off. None of us knew what to do, and this woman comes running from one of the nearby trailers and offers to help. She managed to get the bleeding to stop. But then she disappeared. One of the bystanders—Charlene—found some keys that she thought the lady might have dropped. I went with her to drop them off at the lost and found. Thought maybe the lady might turn up while we were there, and I'd get a chance to say thanks for what she'd done."

Steven nodded. The story was a bit convoluted, but he was following so far. His eye caught Kenny, who was staring at him as if trying to suss him out.

"Anyway," Carl continued. "Word travels real quick around here. Turns out, we were right that the keys belonged to the lady. 'Cause she did come by to get them. And then that's when Dottie Swallows, who was working the lost and found, got it into her head that the little girl she had with her looked like a kid on that Amber Alert. It all happened pretty quick after that. Dottie notified fair security, who contacted the police, but in the meantime, the lady and the kid slipped away. Crazy story, right?"

Steven nodded. Crazy and worrisome. But Etta would be quick to recognize the danger.

And if she thought the police were looking for her, she'd definitely take care. The question was, what could he do to help them?

"Well," he finally said to Carl and Kenny, who were clearly expecting some sort of reaction, "if the lady saved your nephew, it seems unlikely she'd be kidnapping some kid."

"That's what I said," Carl exclaimed.

"Hey, I know who you are!" Kenny interrupted. "You're Steven Hunt! You won the PBR Championship. Twice." His face suddenly fell. "But you got really badly hurt last time you rode, didn't you? Jumping into the ring to help your friend."

Steven inclined his head. "Yep. That's me. But as you can see, I'm pretty much recovered. Not that I'll be climbing on the back of a bull anytime soon. But I sure do miss it. That's why I'm here."

"Wow! Mr. Hunt. It's honor to meet you." Carl seemed equally excited. "I can't believe that you're staying at the campground. You let us know if there's anything we can do for you. My wife would be more than happy to have you over for dinner."

Steven could feel his lips quirk into a smile. This was one of the things he loved about rodeo people. The generosity and kindness of

men like Carl Deering. "That won't be necessary. But I tell you what," he said, deciding to take a gamble, "that girl who helped
your nephew, if you could keep quiet about
her presence here, I think she might appreciate that."

Steven felt the stirrings of unease as a quizzical expression danced across Carl's face.
Maybe he should have stayed mum instead
of taking a chance. Was it his imagination or
did the man have a canny, knowing look in
his eye? Should he try to backpedal and re-
tract his request? It was probably too late for
that. He had already said too much.

"Don't look now, but I think we're about to
have some company…" Kenny's whispered
comment broke through his thoughts. Steven
looked up to see two police officers headed
their way.

NINE

Steven's eyes darted toward his companions, a pit of unease forming in his gut. A knowing smile was twitching on Carl's lips. And, as for Kenny, well, the boy didn't seem to have put two and two together, at least not yet.

The officers were getting closer. Steven's mind scrambled to weigh the options. Should he admit the truth to Carl? Or would that just make it worse? Maybe he should just back away from the group and pretend there was something that required his attention.

"Hey there, folks," a burly officer said. He stepped in front of Steven, blocking his exit.

"What do you want?" Kenny's voice was aggressive.

The thinner, shorter cop gave the boy an amused smile. "We're just asking around to see if anyone has seen a woman with a small child."

Carl chuckled. "We've seen lots and lots of women and children. You're going to have to be a bit more specific than that."

The first officer frowned. "Average height. Short red hair. The kid is about four or five."

"Is she in trouble?" Carl's voice held just a hint of malice.

"At this point, we just want to ask her some questions. We think she may have helped an injured kid earlier today."

"Oh, *that* woman!" Carl seemed to be relishing the attention. "Yeah. I saw the whole thing. She saved my nephew's life. But I don't recall seeing a child with her."

"Hmm." The shorter officer took off his hat and scratched his head. "And you haven't seen her since then? Any of you?"

Steven shook his head. It wasn't even a lie. He hadn't seen Etta or Polly since he'd left to talk to Donny.

"Nah. Nah. I haven't seen her," Carl said, "but there was some young fellow around here who was asking about her."

The office stepped closer. "Really? And did you get the name of this man or have any idea where he was headed?"

"He wasn't from here. That's the reason I'm telling you this. I'm pretty sure that all three shoved off already, though. The man claimed he had come up from El Paso to get some parts for his tractor. You know, you can find great deals at these fairs. One time, my boy Kenny, here, and I were able to get diesel motor for a quarter of its cost just 'cause it was slightly used."

Steven slowly blew out a breath and unclenched his hands. It seemed that Carl wasn't going to give him up. But Etta and Polly had to be stuck somewhere on the fairgrounds, probably waiting for the commotion to die down. Given the police presence and the level of security, that didn't seem likely anytime soon. Which meant that he needed to extricate himself from this conversation and find them immediately. Carl was still rambling on about engines to the taller officer, who, from his follow-up questions, seemed engaged by the subject. Steven cast a quick peek at the other officer. Arms crossed and foot tapping, he clearly wanted to move along.

"Hey, man…" Kenny's voice, previously belligerent and forceful, was soft and discreet when he whispered to Steven. "You may want to head back to your Airstream to check on your woman."

What did that mean? The adrenaline that

had been simmering in Steven's chest again surged through his limbs. Was the kid trying to send him a message? If so, he didn't understand. He scanned the area around them. No sign of Etta or Polly. His eyes flicked toward the boy, who gave the slightest tilt with his head toward a row of picnic tables and grills set about a hundred feet away. Steven squinted in that direction. There weren't too many people around, but maybe one of them could be Etta.

"Well, I guess I better be on my way, then." Steven turned toward the officers. "I hope you find the people you are looking for." Then he turned toward Carl and held out his hand. "Thanks for your help."

"Don't mention it." Carl returned the firm handshake. "You know how it is here in the country. One person needs an egg, you just ask the next campsite over. We look out for each other. Here, take Kenny with you. He's actually planning to make a cake, so maybe he can borrow a couple from you. I'm going to show these officers the new Hemi I just installed in my truck, and Kenny is sick to death of hearing about it. C'mon, fellas, my Chevy is parked over here behind my camper."

Carl headed off toward a large pickup,

still bending the ear of the burly officer. The shorter policeman trailed behind, looking less than pleased.

"She's over there." Kenny started to walk toward the picnic site. But before they reached the tables and grills, the teen veered toward the lavatories. Serious doubts started to form in Steven's mind. Should he trust this kid? Did he even understand that the person the police were looking for was his so-called woman?

"She went in there." Kenny pointed to the door to the ladies' bathroom.

"You're sure?" Steven didn't mean to sound skeptical, but he could hear a tinge of disbelief in his voice. "You saw her go in?"

"I've got good eyes. My mom thinks I should become a pilot because my vision is so sharp, but I want to see how I do on the rodeo circuit first."

"Right." Steven stared at the door with uncertainty. "I guess I better go in."

Kenny smirked.

Really, after everything that he and Etta had been through in the last twenty-four hours, it was ridiculous to be wary of entering the women's bathroom. Still, with Carl distracting the officers, this was his chance to get Etta and Polly back to the Airstream without being caught. With a final sigh, he pushed open the door and stepped inside.

Etta crouched against the ceramic tile of the toilet in the farthest stall. Her arms wrapped tightly around Polly, she squeezed her eyes shut and offered up a silent plea to God. Terror was knotted in her gut as, just moments earlier, she had heard the door to the bathroom swish open and then bang closed. Was it just another woman, coming in to use the facilities? Or was it one of the relentless pack of security officers she and Polly had been dodging for the last forty-five minutes as they made their way back to the Airstream?

The sound of booted footsteps echoed against the floor. Blood pounded in her chest, and she tightened her grip on Polly. *Please, please, God, let us be safe.*

"Etta? Are you in here?" a familiar voice whispered.

Relief flooded her senses. "Steven."

"Yeah. It's me. We need to get you out of here now."

Her fingers trembling, Etta reached up, pushed the lock back and opened the door. At the sight of Steven's familiar face, Etta felt an intense desire to burst into tears. But no. That wouldn't solve anything.

"Here, let me help you." Steven reached in and lifted Polly up into his arms. The little girl stared at him with solemn eyes and then laid her head down on his shoulder as Etta scrambled to her feet.

"He's here, Steven." Etta's voice trembled.

"Who's here?"

"Gray Beard. I heard him when we were in the goat barn. He said I killed a cop."

Steven shook his head. "I'm sure he'd say anything if he thought it would help track you down. But I wish I knew how he found out that you were at the fair. He must have some sort of pipeline to the police."

A gasp stuck in her throat. "Are the police here, too?"

"Yeah. But don't worry. We'll be on the road before they even know we're gone."

Still holding Polly, Steven walked to the door of the lavatory and pushed it open. After the harshness of the fluorescent bulbs, the dusky darkness caught her by surprise, and she blinked for a moment as she took in her surroundings. The coast was clear. No police. No security guards. No gray-bearded man determined to find her. The only people around were a couple of kids roasting hot dogs on a grill.

She sighed with relief.

But a second later, her heart resumed its frenetic pounding in her chest. She had nearly walked straight into a teenager lurking beside the door. He looked at her for a moment and then turned to Steven.

"Dad will keep the cops distracted for a while. That should give you enough time to get back to your camper and be on your way."

Steven nodded. "Thanks, Kenny. You're a good kid."

Etta exhaled in relief. Steven seemed to know this person.

"Where are you parked?" the kid asked.

"About two spots down from you. Donny Gage's trailer."

"I know the one." The boy paused, as if thinking. "You want me to drive it down here, so you can avoid the police?"

"That would be great. Etta, can you give Kenny the keys?"

"Huh? Oh, right. The keys." The cause of all this trouble. Etta reached inside her pocket and fished them out. "You don't look old enough to have a license."

The teenager rolled his eyes. "Ma'am, I've

been driving since I was nine. I'm not exactly official, but, trust me, I'm a good driver."

Etta cast a glance at Steven. He nodded.

Reluctantly, she placed the keys in the boy's outstretched fingers.

"I'll be back as quick as I can," the boy said. "It might take a little while to get everything unplugged and packed up." A moment later, he was bounding away.

"Friend of yours?" Etta asked after a few seconds of silence.

"Seems to be."

"Seems to be?" Etta said, echoing back Steven's words. "What does that mean?"

"Well, I just met him and his dad, so I suppose you can call him a friendly acquaintance."

Steven's offhand manner was beginning to grate on her nerves. "You just met him, and we gave him the keys to the Airstream?"

Steven adjusted his hold on Polly. "Look, you're going to have to trust me on this. If Kenny or his dad were going to turn us in, they've already had the opportunity."

Another silence descended between them as Etta considered what Steven was asking of her. *Trust.* That was something that had never come easy to her. Too many people in her life

had let her down when she needed them most.
Her father. Her mother. Even Lilly during her
delinquent days. Steeling herself against inevitable disappointment had become a survival
technique for most of her life. And when Steven had come to her rescue during the home
invasion, she had initially felt that same sense
of wariness and mistrust. But in the course of
time, Steven had come through for her, risk-
ing his own freedom and doing everything in
his power to keep her and Polly safe.

"I like your hair." Steven's voice interrupted her thoughts.

"Oh." She reached up to touch the short
tresses. "Thanks."

"I heard you saved some little kid's life.
Well done on that."

His praise warmed her. Suddenly embar-
rassed, she turned her gaze away. "Slight ex-
aggeration. I just helped stop the bleeding."

"I figured you had a good reason for leaving the trailer. When I got back and couldn't
find you, I was worried."

"I'm grateful that you found us. I think my
heart actually leapt when I heard you call my
name in the bathroom."

"Glad to be of assistance." He smiled, and
there it was again—that flush of joy along

with the crazy feeling of her heart beating double-time in her chest.

"How did you manage to make it this far without being caught?" he asked.

Where to begin? After hiding with the goats, she and Polly had snuck out and attached themselves to a large family group. That had gotten them as far as the birthing stables. There, they had dodged in and out of buildings and barns, slowly making their way back to the campsite. She gave him the condensed version.

"We just kept to the edge of the crowd and tried to stay hidden," she explained.

"Well, I'm impressed. I wasn't back at the campsite for more than ten minutes before I was pulled into a conversation with two police officers. So, clearly, you have better evasion skills than me."

Etta cast a sharp glance in Steven's direction. Was he being patronizing? No, Steven never said anything he didn't mean. Suddenly, the hairs on the back of her neck started to stand up. Who was that man in khaki shorts over by the picnic benches?

"Steven," she said, lowering her voice to a whisper. "I think that security guard is getting closer."

Steven glanced at the man and nodded. "Right. Maybe you and Polly should go back into the bathroom to hide until Kenny gets here with the Airstream. I'll wander away, so it doesn't look like I am loitering in front of the women's lavatory."

"Shouldn't Kenny have gotten back already? The trailer is close by." Apprehension was again pricking at her brain. She didn't want to question Steven's decision to trust the teenager, but she couldn't help the jolt of uncertainty.

Steven grimaced. "Yeah. But he did have to unplug the connections and whatnot. Actually, I think I see him coming. Yeah, there's the POW flag. It's definitely our ride."

"Good." She hadn't wanted to go back into the bathroom to cower on the floor. She glanced toward the picnic tables. The two security officers were involved in a conversation with the teens at the grill. She turned her gaze back toward the road. She had to concede—the kid was a good driver. On an uneven surface barely wide enough to accommodate the Airstream, Kenny seemed to be having no difficulty navigating the dusty lane.

The RV came to a shuddering halt just a

few feet from the lavatory, and Kenny popped out of the Airstream.

"I left it running. Sorry it took so long. Dad was still talking, but he got a little information from the police as well. Apparently, they're checking vehicles as they leave the fair, but only at the north entrance. They don't have enough officers to cover the other gates yet."

"Right," Steven said, pulling open the side door and setting Polly down to find a seat in the back of the trailer. He turned to face his new friend with a smile. "You and your dad have been a great help, Kenny. Here—" He tugged his cowboy hat, pulled a Sharpie out of his pocket and signed the brim. The kid pulled off his ball cap and replaced it with the Stetson, then offered a half salute and a grin as he walked away.

Etta wished she had something to give him, too.

Steven opened the front door and claimed the seat behind the wheel.

Etta shook her head. "Let's change seats. You're not supposed to be driving."

"I'll be fine. There still could be some sort of security checkpoint, so I should probably sit up front alone while you and Polly hole up where you won't be seen."

She wanted to argue with him, but his logic made sense. Besides, she didn't have any energy left for a fight. She hustled back to the side door and scampered inside. Even before she had pulled the door closed completely, they were on the move.

"C'mon, sweet pea." She held Polly's hand, and they walked toward the back. Would it be reckless to turn on the overhead light? Probably. But sitting in the cramped darkness was too depressing. Willing herself to find the positive, Etta fished around for a blanket and then draped it around Polly's shoulders.

"I think it's time for a story. You already know the one of the three little pigs, but have you ever heard the story of the three little wolves?"

Polly shook her head.

"Well, once upon a time, there were three little wolves…" Etta kept her voice to a soft murmur, hoping her lilting tone would help lull Polly to sleep. She could tell from the vibrations below her feet that they were still on a dirt road. Then, there came a sudden, jerking stop. Etta cut off the story and held her breath. It seemed like at least three minutes passed, but finally the Airstream began moving again. She looked down at Polly. The little girl had fallen asleep.

Etta adjusted Polly's position on the pull-out bed, tucking the blanket around her, and then peeked out from behind the partition. All appeared clear.

Once they'd exited the fairgrounds, she slid into the passenger seat next to Steven and offered him her best smile. "What do you think of heading to Sulphur Springs where we can find a place to pull in for the night? Tomorrow morning, we can see if we can arrange to visit with Jordan Shapiro."

TEN

The brass plate in the center of the town house's front door was very discreet. Jordan Shapiro. Private Investigator. Discreet Inquiries Welcome.

When they left the fairgrounds in Leesburg, Etta had been adamant that they needed to head straight for Sulphur Springs. But Jordan's office hours didn't begin until ten o'clock the next day, so they had driven to a nearby Walmart lot where they had spent the night.

Now, after two trips around the block, counting back and forward, looking for the address, they had finally found the right place. But it remained to be seen whether or not this additional detour would yield information that would be worth the risk.

Steven locked eyes with Etta, who was standing beside him, holding hands with Polly. He shifted his gaze toward the high-tech camera, its black lens focused on the threshold.

"I saw it, too," Etta muttered under her breath, taking a step sideways and turning her head.

"Not a great start to our adventure. But ready or not, here we go." He lifted his hand and rang the bell above the mail slot.

A few minutes passed before a prim, older woman in a fitted blue suit opened the door. She seemed more annoyed than intrigued to see them waiting on the front steps. "I assume you're here to see Jordan. Do you have an appointment?"

Steven nodded. "Yes, of course. Matt Bickler of Thompson, Colfax, and Bickler." His white lie caused Etta to flinch as she waited beside him. While it was true that the voicemail message he'd left a half hour earlier had been a bit fuzzy on details, he had correctly estimated their arrival time to be around ten o'clock. He pointed at his watch. Three minutes early. Perfect.

The woman disappeared, returning a few moments later, a deep frown creasing her forehead. "Jordan just saw your message, and she apologizes for the inconvenience. But she's extremely busy at the moment, and she won't be able to see you today. Would you like to reschedule for next week?"

Steven shook his head. "We're only in town for a few hours, so now is our only option."

"I'm sorry, Mr. Bickler. But 'now' is just not possible."

"I understand. But perhaps you would ask Ms. Shapiro if she could spare just a couple of minutes to talk to the sister of an old friend," he pleaded. "We're willing to wait for as long as it takes."

The stylish woman disappeared inside once again, this time pulling the door shut behind her.

"She's not going to see us," Etta whispered. "Maybe it was a waste of time coming all this way."

"Let's see what happens," Steven said. As they waited, he snuck another glance at Etta. With her short, very red haircut and oversize glasses, she reminded him of the confident girl he had fallen in love with years ago.

He pulled his gaze away. This wait felt like an eternity. Out of the corner of his eye, he checked out the CCTV recording device above them in the entryway. Was someone inside watching their every move? No doubt, the camera had already captured a full-on shot of all three waiting on the threshold.

At long last, the door swished open. Gone was the older woman in the blue suit. In her place was a younger, spandex-clad female with spiked pink hair.

"Yes? What do you want, then? I believe my assistant already explained that I have no openings, but, apparently, you won't take no for an answer."

"Ms. Shapiro?" Steven asked. "We were hoping to talk to you about Lilly Sanderson, or Lilly Mitchell, as you knew her in the past."

The woman's face darkened. "Lilly's dead. I have nothing to say on the subject."

"Maybe not," Steven said, "but surely you can take a moment or two to answer a couple of questions about the situation."

"Fine." The woman pulled the door open wider. "But I only have a very small window of time before my next appointment. I suppose you better come inside."

A few minutes later, Steven found himself sitting next to Etta and Polly on a white leather couch in a small office. Modern art graced the ivory walls, and hundreds of hardcover books were stacked in untidy piles throughout the space. Seated behind a glass desk, Jordan Shapiro tented her arms and leaned forward, training her gaze on Steven.

"My assistant tells me that your name is Matt Bickler. And I recognize your companions from pictures on Lilly's Facebook page—her daughter Polly and her sister Etta with drastically different hair."

Steven cleared his throat. So, much for the efficacy of Etta's new look. But, whatever. They had the Airstream now, so there would be no need for her to venture out in public. And, on the plus side, Jordan's claim to familiarity gave them a logical place to start.

"Cards on the table here since we don't have much time. We know that you and Lilly were friends. And we know for a fact that she had reached out to you about some sort of scheme that was going to make her rich."

"You know for a fact, huh? I don't like talking to lawyers, Mr. Bickler, especially when they choose to adopt a confrontational tone."

"Perhaps I should explain," Etta interjected. "Matt is part of a team representing Lilly's husband Greg who has been arrested for her murder."

"So, Lilly's daughter has become your ward?"

"I'm taking care of her, yes. But only until Greg is proven innocent."

"How old are you, kid?" Jordan turned her attention to Polly.

No answer.

"Shy. I get it. Your mama taught you not to talk to strangers. Smart lady." Jordan turned her gaze back to Etta. "I seem to remember that she's around five, am I right? Maybe old enough to have learned some facts from watching her mother."

"What Polly knows isn't the issue," Steven interjected. "We understand that Lilly reached out to you before her death. We have no idea what that was about, just that it was something big. We're not saying that it's anything illegal. But her connection to you is one of the few credible leads we have at the moment. So if you know anything at all that can help us understand what or who Lilly was investigating, we'd appreciate you sharing it with us today."

Jordan blew out a long sigh. "Okay, listen. Against my better judgment, I'm going to tell you what I know. But don't get your hopes up that it's going to break open the case against her husband Greg. According to the papers, the evidence appears to be stacked against him."

"But…"

Jordan held up a hand to forestall Etta's question. "I first heard from Lilly in January. She claimed she was on the verge of making a huge score. Same old Lilly. Always thinking she was smarter than everyone else. Sorry," Jordan said, looking at Etta and Polly. "She was my friend but she sometimes acted a little too self-pleased. Anyway, she told me that she had stumbled across something that has the potential to be a major game changer. What that is exactly, she wouldn't say. 'A blast from the past' was how she described it at the time. I remember how she was always so fascinated by true crime stories in juvie, and I knew she had a part-time gig reporting and wanted to make it big. If I had to guess, I'd say that her big scoop involved something like that. But that's all I know."

"But that was your first contact," Steven pressed. "We know that you heard from her more than once. Did she offer any explanation as to why what she was working on was top secret?"

Jordan shot him a look. Clearly, she preferred Etta's gentle inquiries to his pointed questions. "No names. No details. I told you. Lilly didn't like to share. And I've learned to be discreet as well. I did offer her advice about protecting the data she had gathered in the course of her investigation. Nothing specific. Can't you pull these details from her computer or cell?"

Etta shook her head. "There was nothing on her hard drive. The police checked into that."

"See what I mean?" Jordan held up her hands in resignation. "She was paranoid about anyone uncovering her secrets." She paused for a moment and then continued, "We spoke again in mid-February, and she claimed that she was close to reeling in a big fish. I told her to be careful and keep a record of everything she found out. That made her giggle in that crazy way I remember from the time we spent together in juvie." Jordan smiled momentarily. "She told me not to worry, that she'd downloaded her notes on a USB that was tucked away in a spot where it wouldn't be found. Said that she has a kid now and caution is her middle name. That's it. I was out of the country on an extended vacation for most of March and half of April. And when I got home, I heard she was dead."

"Thank you… You've been very helpful." Steven saw Etta trace a glance from him to

Polly. "Um… Matt, would you mind stepping out for a moment? I have one last question for Jordan."

Steven pulled himself up and turned to face Polly. He had a good idea of what Etta wanted to ask, but he wasn't sure she'd get the answer she was expecting.

"C'mon, kid. How about we wait for your aunt Etta out in the hall?"

As the door of the office quietly slid closed, Jordan made a show of looking at her watch. "Tick tock, Etta. I agreed to meet with you because I genuinely cared about your sister. But there isn't anything more I can say. I just wish I hadn't said those things in front of the kid. I know from the things that Lilly posted that she loved her daughter very much."

Inexplicably, Etta felt her eyes fill with tears. What Jordan said was true. Lilly would have walked across fire for Polly, so whatever she was up to in her investigation, the end result would have benefited Polly in some way.

"I know you don't have much time to chat," Etta began, "but I did want to ask you one thing. You said you were out of the country when Lilly got killed. But when you heard what had happened, did you realize that you had evidence you ought to be sharing with the police?"

Jordan shot her a withering look. "Of course, I did. But when I thought about it, I decided there wasn't much to tell. All I knew was that Lilly had some sort of scoop. I didn't have any specific information."

"Maybe you were also thinking—" Etta had to force herself to be brave "—that you might want to cash in on it for yourself."

"I won't even grace that remark with an answer. And, honestly, Etta. You ought to be more circumspect about tossing out accusations since you yourself are currently on the wrong side of the law."

Etta's chest tightened.

"Did you really think I would agree to meet with you without checking out your credentials? I am a PI, after all. And your story has been front-page news. The short red hair and fake glasses were a momentary distraction, but hey, I'm not about to bust you on this. At least not today. Tomorrow will be time enough to contact the authorities and tell them about your visit. Sorry, Etta, but I don't have a choice. I knew I was walking a thin line by not notifying the authorities about Lilly's attempts to reach out to me. But this is a lot more serious. I could lose my license for withholding information about a fugitive from the police."

Jordan walked across the room and opened the office door. "No hard feelings, eh? It is good to finally meet you, Etta. You remind me of Lilly in all the best ways. Even in the small things, like the way she tilted her head to the side before asking a question that she had no right to know." The woman sighed. "You were a great sister to Lilly while she was in juvie. All those amazing packages you sent full of chocolate bars and the newest books on the bestseller list. I owe you for that, too. And that's the reason I'm giving you a twenty-four-hour head start before I talk to the police. And tell your friend—Matt Bickler, is it?—that I don't plan to share the CCTV footage with the cops. Once you're gone, the tape will be erased, and the system set to reboot. Consider that another gift in honor of Lilly. Take care, Etta. And watch over that kid."

Etta paused on the threshold. She had one more question to ask Jordan, and it was a difficult one to voice. But knowing the state of her sister's finances, she was hoping the PI could offer a small bit of reassurance about Lilly's motives. "This may be impossible for you to answer, but do you think my sister intended to use her information as blackmail?"

Jordan shrugged. "The Lilly I knew was clearly capable of that. But she had a kid to consider. I honestly don't know. There's a chance she was planning to write some sort of tell-all article or book about whatever it was she'd been digging into. I can see how that might get her into trouble, especially if the person she was investigating didn't want that information out there."

Etta stepped out into the hall, and Jordan closed the office door behind her. Hovering in the shadows was Jordan's assistant, who then led her toward the entryway.

There was sympathy in the woman's eyes as she held open the front door. "Your friends said they'd wait for you outside."

"Thanks," Etta said. She rushed down the front steps of the town house and around the corner, where they had left the Airstream. She opened the driver's door and climbed inside, turning to take in the sight of Steven and Polly playing checkers at the table.

"Batten down the game pieces," she said, gunning the motor. "We need to get out of here—now."

A few minutes later, Steven took a seat next

to Etta. "What's the rush? It will take a few minutes for me to pull up the map. What did Jordan say when you accused her of trying to profit off Lilly's investigation?"

In spite of herself, Etta grinned. "How did you know that was what I wanted to talk to her about?"

He shrugged. "It's what I would have asked if I thought I could have gotten away with it. Good call in sending me out with Polly, though. The conversation was getting pretty heavy for her to hear." He glanced back at Polly, who was settled with a book, and added, "But she seemed okay when we got back to the trailer, and she was happy to play a few games of checkers. Danged if she didn't beat me two out of three, though. When that kid finally starts talking, I want to be around to hear what she has to say."

Etta shook her head. "Jordan is planning to report us to the police. She claims to be giving us twenty-four hours head start to get out of town. But she did promise to erase the CCTV footage from the camera at the front door." Etta was glad they'd parked around the corner from the town house. That was one less way they could be tracked.

Steven pulled his phone from his pocket

and peered at the screen. "Clearly, we need to get out of Dodge—I mean, Sulphur Springs—as quickly as possible. I'm thinking it will take around fifteen hours for us to get to the ranch if I take a turn behind the wheel."

She opened her mouth to protest, but he shook his head. "No argument. But I promise we can switch it up if my leg starts to hurt."

Etta glanced at Steven, trying to gauge his reaction to what she was about to say. "I was actually going to suggest a quick stop in Silver Creek."

"Why?" His voice contained an edge of disbelief.

"You heard Jordan say that Lilly downloaded her information to a USB. So now we know what we're looking for." She knew it. This was evidence that would finally crack Lilly's murder case—the truth about what her sister was working on and why she was killed.

"You've got to be kidding, Etta." She could tell he was fighting for calm. "It's a big house. And Greg and the police have both already searched it thoroughly. Even if we make it inside without anyone noticing, it's a dangerous move. And keep in mind that we're talking about a thumb drive. A two-inch gizmo that could be hidden anywhere."

Etta shrugged. Obviously, it would be hard to find. But Steven was forgetting that she had an advantage over Greg and the police. She knew how her sister's mind worked, the way Lilly saw things and looked at the world.

Steven ran his hand through his short hair. "I'm kind of confused here, Etta. I thought the goal was protecting Polly. How can you not recognize the risk in what you're suggesting? If we get caught, you could land in prison. Tell me. How would that help Polly?"

"We can't give up now when we're this close." Etta's voice shook with emotion. She owed it to Lilly to see this through. She hadn't been a great sister these last couple of years, and this was her chance to make things right, to find the evidence and justice for her sister and for Greg. "The final piece of the puzzle is out there, just beyond reach. I can feel it in my heart."

He shook his head. "I still don't think it's a good move. We should be heading to the ranch stat. My brother can help us, and we can continue our investigation. But we'll be doing it from a safe place."

"I hear what you're saying, and I understand that you have qualms about what I'm suggesting. But…"

"Qualms, Etta? I'd say my objections are a bit more serious than qualms. Going back to that house is the last thing we should be doing if the goal is protecting Polly."

"I disagree. And, no matter what you decide, I'm determined to see this through, even if it means doing it on my own. Go big, or go home."

"That's exactly what I've been saying, Etta. In South Dakota we'll find a safe haven at my home."

A deep sadness overwhelmed her senses. Since entering the fray and saving her life during the home invasion in Silver Creek, Steven had been at her side every step in the way. But as a team, they had come full circle in their quest to find the truth about Lilly's murder, and her heart hurt at the thought of setting off on her own. Maybe she'd hire a lawyer to help her once she had the evidence. It wouldn't be easy but she'd figure it out. She looked over at Steven and forced a smile. "We knew all along that our partnership was temporary. I'm grateful for your help and for everything you've done for me and Polly along the way. Given the circumstances, I'm actually surprised you didn't bail sooner."

ELEVEN

"End of the road? What does that mean?" Steven's tone was sharp, almost cutting. "Are you going to abandon me at the bus stop while you and Polly drive the Airstream to Silver Creek? And what's all this about being surprised that I hadn't bailed already? Isn't that your specialty? I mean, you're the one who quit on us."

Etta winced. She had known that she'd gone too far almost as soon as the words left her mouth. She allowed a brief moment of silence to pass before offering a defense. "What I meant to say was that Polly and I have been nothing but trouble these past few days, and almost everyone I know would have left us a long time ago."

Steven cast a long look in her direction. "Sounds like you have the wrong kind of friends."

"Look," she began, trying again. "When Lilly's body was found, the house was also ransacked. Which means that the killer was searching for something, right?"

"Why are you so certain that he didn't find it?"

"Maybe he did. Maybe going back for a second look will just be a colossal waste of time. But if it's still there, I can find it. I know my sister. When she was four, a neighbor gave her five lollipops, and she hid them all in different places throughout our house. Eventually, I found them all, even the one Scotch-taped to her mattress when I was changing the sheets on her bed."

"So Lilly was really good at hiding things. It sounds like you're making my point."

"Yes… I mean no. You're deliberately mis-understanding me."

"Etta, I'm not. I care about you, and I'm just trying to make you see reason. Maybe claiming that you understand Lilly's mindset helps you feel connected to her. But, over the years, she changed, and so did you."

Steven was right about that. Lilly had changed…but in a good way. And even if he had correctly nailed her motives, that wasn't a reason to give up.

"But what's the endgame for me and Polly if we don't discover Lilly's secret? Greg goes to jail and then what? I know you're all in on trying to protect us. But how long can we hide out at your family's ranch? Five years? Ten? Maybe until Polly's old enough to go to college? We can't run forever. And every day we let pass, clues that will help solve Lilly's murder might disappear."

"Can you give me a little credit here?" Steven shifted in his seat. "All I'm saying is that we need to get somewhere safe where we can put our heads together and try to figure this whole thing out."

"But how can we do that if we don't have a clue about a motive for the murder? Everything you say sounds so reasonable, but without any idea of what Lilly was working on, where do we even start? We need to find the USB and see what is on it."

A tap on her shoulder interrupted their argument. Etta turned in her seat to see Polly standing behind them holding a piece of paper. "Hi, sweetheart. Did you draw a picture?" Etta took just a second to glance away from the road. "Oh, it is a flower. Pretty." It was quite a nice drawing for a five-year-old, with purple petals and dark green leaves. But what really pulled at Etta's heartstrings were the painstakingly written-out letters, *P O L L Y*, printed at the top of the page. "I didn't know you could write your name."

Polly pushed the paper toward her.

"Is it for me? Thank you, sweetie. I'm going to set it right here." She propped it up on the dashboard. That seemed to satisfy Polly, who headed to her seat in the back. An uneasy silence settled between her and Steven. Etta felt an itch to continue the discussion. But something told her that Steven needed a break.

Yet a few minutes later, he was the one who brought the subject back up. "If we do this, it will have to be when it's dark out, obviously."

Etta nodded.

"And we'll need to go in with flashlights and be really quick."

Etta nodded again.

"In and out, twenty minutes, tops. No stopping to grab clothes or books or toys for Polly."

Twenty minutes. That wasn't a lot of time. But it was better than nothing.

"Thank you, Steven." She placed a hand on his arm. "We really would be lost without you. Well, I'd be in jail, and Polly would be in foster care. Or worse."

"And," Steven said, pressing his point, "as

soon as we finish our search, we're driving to South Dakota. No more excuses. No more delays."

"Agreed," Etta concurred. She had no desire to stick around at the house any longer than necessary.

Steven took a turn behind the wheel so that she could make a list of Lilly's favorite hiding places. There were a lot of them.

They pulled into a deserted park for dinner—salad and chicken sandwiches from Chick-fil-A—and settled back on folding chairs next to the Airstream to watch the sunset. Both Polly and Steven dozed off, but Etta felt too keyed up to settle down. This could be a make-it-or-break-it moment in solving Lilly's murder. She didn't have a choice. She had to find that USB.

As the sun set, they packed up their stuff and made the short drive to Silver Creek. Steven pulled into a spot a half block away from the address on Dogwood Drive.

Etta headed to the back of the Airstream and kneeled down next to her niece. "Polly... we're going back to your house because we're looking for something. We're not going to turn the lights on, but we'll have flashlights. And we have to be really quiet. Okay?"

As Polly's eyes darkened with fear, Etta felt a chill go through her own body. Maybe Steven was right. Returning to the scene of the crime was too big of a gamble. The memory of the body of the man she had killed, lying inert in the hall, flashed across her brain, but she blinked it away. She needed to stay strong. They could do this. No one would see them as they crept under the cover of darkness down past the other homes on Dogwood Drive. And once they were inside the house, the rest would be easy. Relying on her sisterly instincts, she would quickly find the USB.

That was the plan.

She glanced over at Steven. He had slipped on a hoodie from Walmart and was standing by the Airstream's door. "Ready to go?"

Etta pulled in a long breath. She looked at Polly, whose face was a mask of terror. And as the implications of what they were about to do hit her, all of her resolve evaporated, and she realized that there was no way that she could take this child back into that house. And she couldn't for one minute leave her alone.

"Steven," she said, her voice tentative and soft enough for only him to hear. "I've changed my mind. I can't do this, not with Polly."

Steven nodded. "Okay. Give me the key and your list, and I'll do the search?"

"No." She shook her head. Steven's kind gesture touched her heart, and it was tempting to take him up on the offer. But he didn't know Lilly. Even with her list of possible hiding places, he would have no idea where she would have tucked away the USB. "I should be the one who goes into the house while you stay back with Polly. We're here, anyway, so I might follow this lead to its logical conclusion. I'll be fine—I promise. It won't take long. A half hour, tops."

"Etta, after what happened before with the intruder, I don't think…" Steven's eyes were clouded with worry.

"I know you'd rather be the one to take the lead on this, but it has to be me. I can do this. I can be brave like you, or at least I can try." She reached out and touched his hand, holding his gaze for a moment, and then she was out the door.

She had to dig deep for an extra spot of courage as the hundred-yard trek to the house felt interminable. Every sound seemed amplified by the darkness. Her footsteps seemed too noticeable. Her breathing too loud. With trembling fingers, she inserted the key into the latch. But the handle refused to turn. Had someone changed the locks? The blood that had already been pounding in her chest intensified in its beat.

She fumbled with the lock twice more, jigging the key and pressing down even harder on the handle. Her hammering heart slowed its frantic pulsing as the door swung open and she stepped inside.

Upstairs first. She'd save the kitchen for last. The memories of the attack there still lingered in her mind.

She flicked on her flashlight. With twenty minutes to go and counting, she took the steps two at a time.

She'd start in the bathroom. Lilly had always liked to hide things with her makeup. She opened the top drawer on the vanity and rolled the beam of light across a tangle of necklaces, but there was no sign of a thumb drive. Onto the bottom drawer, which contained only a half-dozen tubes of lipstick and mascara.

She continued to check off the hiding spots on her list, but she kept coming up short. A knot of frustration tightened in her chest as she realized that a quarter of an hour had passed, and all she had proven was how little she knew of her sister.

But she wasn't ready to give up yet. She headed down the steps into the kitchen, her eyes scanning the shelf above the sink and settling on an African violet, now parched and droopy, on the windowsill.

Suddenly, it clicked. The drawing Polly had shown them in the Airstream. Was it possible that she trying to show them where Lilly had stashed the USB?

She set the plant on the counter and began to dig, her heart pounding. The soil was dry, almost hardened by the lack of water, but she clawed and sifted through it with her fingers. She touched something hard, so she dug a little deeper. When she pulled her hand out of the dirt, clenched in her palm was a two-inch thumb drive. She brushed off the loose soil clinging to the case and slipped it into her pocket.

She pulled in a deep breath and enjoyed a moment of elation. But it was short-lived.

The click of the front door opening echoed through the hall and sent her senses into over-drive.

Was it Steven? Had he left Polly alone in the Airstream and headed to the house to see what was taking her so long? No. She had been gone for less than twenty minutes. Not enough time had passed to cause him to panic.

At least not yet.

Voices echoed in the hall. There seemed to be two—or maybe three—intruders. Too many for her to take on alone. Panic threatened to overwhelm her. How was it possible that the men had found her here alone?

But she refused to give in to the paralyzing fear engulfing her senses. She scanned the kitchen. Where were the knives? Or that cast-iron skillet? There had to be something—anything—she could use as a weapon. But the men in the hall were getting closer, and there wasn't time to reach the back door.

Her gaze landed on the broom closet a few feet away. It was barely wide enough to fit a pail of cleaning supplies and a dustpan. But if she stood on top of the bucket and held her breath, she might be able to squeeze inside. But what to do then? She'd be trapped with no chance of escape, and no idea at all about what was going on. But what was the alternative? She slipped inside and pulled the door closed in the nick of time.

Heavy footsteps sounded against the kitchen floor, followed by the slamming of cabinets and clattering of silverware in drawers. The intruders appeared to be looking for something, not someone. And considering the sounds drifting through the closet door, it was probably something small.

As small as a thumb drive? It was certainly possible that Greg had shared his concerns about Lilly's investigative work with Sam Colfax, who had, deliberately or accidentally, passed on the information to his colleagues at the firm. Well, even if the intruders found her, Etta wasn't going to make it easy for them to claim the USB. She twisted open the upper casing of her flashlight and dropped the small device inside, next to the bulb. Then she reassembled the mechanism and slipped it back into her pocket as she waited for the next shoe to drop.

The intruder's footsteps were closer now. Etta imagined him stopping inches from her hiding place, deciding whether or not to check the closet. She held the knob tight as he pulled and twisted, doing his part to win the tug-of-war. One final, hard yank, and she lost her grip, and a shaft of light flooded the closet, revealing the face of a burly man who had the presence of mind to reach inside and cuff her wrists.

"Well, this is a surprise. Hey, Mike," he called out. "Come and see what I found!"

Her heart plummeted in her chest as Mike appeared at the kitchen door. Even with his long gray beard masking most of his features, she could see the sly grin on his lips.

"Nice find, Pete." Mike—or Gray Beard, as she had been calling him—cackled with delight. "Henrietta Mitchell, I assume. Funny thing. We've been looking for you everywhere. Little did we know that if we had just waited, you would have come to us."

Gone was the chatty neighbor, concerned about her state of mind. In his place was an angry and formidable foe. "TJ's going to be pleased," he said in a voice that was laced with menace. "Get upstairs and tell Doug about the change of plans. We're looking for the kid, who's probably hiding somewhere in the house. Find her, and we've solved all our problems."

Mike gave her a menacing smile as Pete headed up the stairs. "You've caused us a great deal of trouble," he said in a threatening tone. She shrank away from her assailant, into the shadows, but only long enough to grab the first spray bottle she could reach on the shelf of cleaning supplies. She squirted

it into the man's eyes. Mike stumbled backward, and she gave him a hard shove before
skidding away through the patio door.

She had only a small head start. But it was
dark and she knew the lay of the land. She
knew she wouldn't make it to the gate in time,
so she climbed inside the storage unit along
the back patio wall, bending her knees until
they were almost touching her face and pulling the lid closed on top.

The kitchen door slammed open, and the
tread of heavy boots could be heard against
the concrete patio. Then silence. Hardly dar-
ing to breathe, she imagined her pursuer looking to the right and the left, trying to decide
which way she had gone.

An electric buzzing split the air, followed
by a loud groan of pain.

"Are you there, Etta?" a voice whispered.
"It's me. Steven."

With her free hand, she pushed aside the
container's lid. "I'm here," she said. As she
climbed out of the bin, her eyes were drawn
to the spot where Gray Beard was lying,
twitching on the patio floor.

Steven reached over and took her hand.
"That Taser jolt I hit him with won't last long.
We need to get out of here as fast as we can."

TWELVE

The city lights of each passing town disappeared into a darkness broken only by the occasional green highway sign pointing bleakly to a crossroad ahead. Highway I-35 streamed like a smooth ribbon between Dallas and Oklahoma City, an easy drive if Steven could ignore the occasional twinge in his right leg. It would be nearly dawn before they reached Kansas and put the South behind them on their journey home.

But he was getting ahead of himself. They had miles to go before they reached South Dakota and the safety of his family's ranch. He exhaled in relief, reveling in the fact that they had made it this far and that Etta was okay.

He shot a glance at her. She was curled up on the passenger seat beside him. Was it his imagination, or was she looking extra beautiful with her hair all tousled and that flush in her cheeks?

"You sure you're not hurt in any way?"

"Absolutely," she said. "Thanks to you."

No. He had to give this one to God. He had been waiting in the Airstream, checking the time, when he was struck by a sudden conviction that he needed to see what was happening at the house. Polly was fast asleep, and even though Etta hadn't been gone long enough to cause him to worry, he couldn't shake the feeling that something was wrong. And grabbing the Taser from the glove compartment on his way out the door proved to be a key decision. As was the fact that Etta had been able to hide from the man pursuing her. Gray Beard, she called him, though they now knew his real name was Mike. She had gotten names and descriptions of another as well— Pete. She hadn't seen the one named Doug, or the man who hadn't been at the house but who seemed to be in charge of the operation, this mysterious TJ.

He snuck another glance at Etta. Maybe, after everything they had been through thus far on their journey, now would be a good time to have the talk they had been avoiding since he'd first arrived at Lilly and Greg's house. When he had taken her hand on their sprint toward the Airstream, in his instinct to protect her, he'd felt a jolt of a longing for what was once between them. And he had wondered...had Etta felt it, too?

It was hard to say. It seemed that she did want to talk tonight, but not about her feelings. She wanted to discuss what he thought the men had been doing at the house.

"They were looking for something, too. Do you think Greg told Sam Colfax that you visited him at the prison?"

He shrugged. "I asked him not to mention it, but at this point, we have no way of knowing what he said."

"But we have the evidence now, so we can find out for sure."

"We sure do. I can't believe the thumb drive was in the plant like the one Polly drew. Even so, it was touch and go there for a moment."

"Mmm-hmm," Etta agreed. Which seemed like a mild reaction to the fact that she had been moments away from being discovered hiding. And if she had been caught... He didn't even want to think about it. What he wanted to think about was the sensation of Etta's fingers entwined with his as they'd run toward the Airstream. "What do you think is on the USB?" she asked.

He shrugged again. "I'm not sure. Ideally, it will be information that will lead us to Lilly's killer."

"Huh," Etta replied. Clearly, she was hoping for a more prolonged discussion.

But he wasn't willing to engage in idle speculation. They needed to wait until they reached the ranch and logged into a secure network. Then, there was a good chance that many of their questions would be answered.

"Are you getting tired? Want me to drive?" she asked.

"I'm good for at least another half hour or so. Is Polly still asleep?"

Etta craned her next to check the back of the Airstream. "Out like a light. She's really been a trooper, all things considered." She was quiet for a moment and then picked up a thread of an old conversation. "Do you think what Lilly was doing was on the up-and-up?"

What she meant was…do you think my sister got killed because she tried to blackmail the wrong person? But he wasn't going to touch that one with a ten-foot pole.

Etta continued. "Maybe she really was writing some sort of éxposé. But if she was trying to extort money from whoever it was that she was investigating, it would have been a good motive for murder. And it would explain a lot about these people who are after us. But I have a hard time imagining that she would have risked the life she had made with Greg and Polly."

"Maybe she didn't see what she was doing as a risk. Maybe she felt like she had it all under control."

"Yeah. Jordan was right in what she said about Lilly. That she always tended to act like she was the smartest person in the room."

Steven nodded, surprised that Etta was able to recognize that about her sister. He hadn't known, until Greg mentioned it, that Lilly had spent time in juvie. But he wasn't at all surprised. "You said that she changed and became a great mother and wife, but I'm still kind of ticked off at her right now. Whether it was blackmail or some more legit scheme, she's the cause of this whole mess. No matter how you look at it, she should have taken her information to the police."

"But..."

He shook his head. "She should have been smart enough to know the risks. Now Greg's in jail and Lilly isn't talking. And you're on the run as a fugitive."

Etta shot a glance at him. "And you're implicated for helping me and Polly."

"I'm not worried about that, Etta."

Etta shook her head. "You're right about Lilly being jealous of the time you and I spent together. But, you know, despite all her faults, she helped me sort through a lot of the anger I felt toward my mother. She gave me a Bible and taught me forgiveness and how to pray. Funny. In most families, it's the other way around. The older sister leading the younger one. But not for us. It was all Lilly."

"Well, I'm glad to hear that. But that doesn't take away from the fact that your sister got caught up in something that was more than she could control."

Etta nodded. "That's true. But she shouldn't be blamed because things didn't work out between us."

"I agree," he said, tapping his brake as the semi in front of him slowed for a turn.

"Good. Because it's important that you recognize that we broke up for reasons that have nothing to do my sister's manipulations."

"Why do I need to realize that?" he wanted to know.

"Because we're here now, on the way to the ranch. I assume your family knows that we once dated. Or maybe they don't. I guess I shouldn't make assumptions."

"They know."

"Okay, then. So what if your mom asks what caused the break-up?"

"I guarantee that there is no way she is going to ask you that."

"But what if she does? What should I tell her? Should I mention that you thought my sister was a brat? Or, shall I describe the way you asked me to marry you?"

He glanced back at her. Were they really going to do this now? Apparently they were, since all of a sudden, Etta seemed extremely fired up by the subject.

"Okay, Etta. I give up. I can see you have a lot to say on this particular subject. Tell me, then. What was so awful about the way I proposed?"

"Let's just say that I wasn't thrilled to have such a private, romantic moment captured on the jumbotron at a Rangers game during the seventh-inning stretch."

"You said yes."

"Of course, I did. The entire stadium was applauding and shouting for me to take the ring. I had to smile and act like I was happy. Anything else would have been humiliating for both of us." Etta shook her head. "C'mon, Steven. I realize that at that point, we had only known each other for a short time, but, even so, you should have understood that kind of public spectacle wasn't my style."

Indignation pulsed through his veins. "I guess that explains why you changed your mind the next day."

She shrugged. "Well, that wasn't the only thing. It just caused me to realize that we didn't know each other well enough to make a lifelong commitment."

He scratched his head. His short haircut was just at the very beginning of growing in, and his scalp felt itchy and uncomfortable. Then again, maybe it was just the direction that the conversation seemed to be taking.

"So what was the real reason you had for turning me down? You better go ahead and tell me. Because, I've got to say, this stuff about you not liking my proposal is all coming as a complete surprise to me. When you handed me back my ring you claimed that you couldn't get married because you needed to care for Lilly until she finished high school and that you had plans to work as a traveling nurse. You claimed that was your dream, and I believed you."

"It *was* my dream." She turned toward him. "Obviously, since that was what I did after you left. And it's what I'm still doing today. Look, I admit that we left a lot of things unsaid when we broke up. The way it went down was so raw and filled with emotion. And even though I knew that our getting married at that point would be a big mistake, it didn't mean that I didn't care."

He shrugged. "So you cared about me, and once upon a time you even claimed that you loved me. But you didn't want to spend the rest of your life with me?"

Etta nodded.

"Wow. Okay, then. I guess I always thought that the way we felt about each other would be enough to get us through any rough patches along the way. But you know what, Etta? I'm actually glad I didn't know about any of this at the time. It might have been hard to deal with the fact that I was a complete dope to think that having twenty thousand people cheering at the idea of us tying to knot was romantic."

She let out a breath. "You are deliberately misconstruing what I've been trying to say.

Let me try again. Do you remember telling me that you wanted to take me away from my 'dysfunctional life'?"

He shook his head. "I don't."

"Well, you did. And I knew that by that you meant Lilly. You thought I needed to be rescued. But I finally had my nursing degree and Lilly was almost old enough to be on her own. I told you. I had plans. Maybe they weren't as exciting as a bull-riding career, but they were mine."

"That's not fair." He glanced at her. "I never expected you to follow me around the country watching me compete. I knew you had your own career. I just thought that once we decided to get married, we'd have a conversation about how to make it all work out."

"You didn't say that, Steven." Etta's voice was low, almost a whisper. "Maybe you planned to mention it later, but there wasn't the chance. You walked away from me, and, until a few days ago, I never saw you again. I always thought that…" She trailed off.

He looked over again. Even in the darkness, he could see that she was crying.

"What, Etta? What did you think?" he asked.

She sniffled and took a moment to pull herself together. "I guess I thought that eventually, you'd reach out to talk. But you didn't. You just rode off into the sunset, and that was it. End of discussion. Case closed. It was hard for a while, knowing I had trusted you with my heart. But then I started to realize that it all worked out for the best. And even now, I really do believe that. Don't you?"

Etta waited for Steven to respond, but he didn't. He just kept his focus on the road ahead.

That realization about them had gotten her through a lot of hard times in the days and months after he left. It took time, but she had successfully convinced herself that their breakup had been a positive thing that had allowed her to keep moving ahead. Once in a while, she'd needed to remind herself of that, when she was feeling lonely or blue. But in time, she got to the point where months went by when she didn't even think about Steven or wonder what he was doing. So why, all of a sudden, was she baiting him into agreeing that he felt that way, too?

But if she had been expecting Steven to claim that he wished that they had done things differently, it didn't seem like it was going to happen. The firm set of his jaw and his hard stare out the window of the Airstream made it clear that he wasn't willing to go there. And how could she blame him? She had just come right out and claimed that their breakup was a good thing, and that she was better off alone.

But was she? She trusted Steven with her life. But it was a different story when it came to her heart.

She settled back against her seat and closed her eyes, determined to rest so that she would be alert for her turn behind the wheel. But sleep didn't come, no matter how hard she tried. She rolled on one side and pressed her head against the cool glass of the window. Two minutes later, she swung up her legs onto the seat, turning toward the front of the vehicle. When that didn't work, she shifted again, this time facing the driver's side. That was the death knell to any hope of slumber as she saw Steven's tense profile glaring straight ahead.

She cleared her throat. "Steven?"

"Yeah?" His tone was hard. Maybe he assumed that she wanted to continue their previous conversation, but he needn't worry about that. She had said all that she wanted to say. "What would you say to taking a break and letting me take a turn behind the wheel?"

A pause. "Okay" was his monosyllabic answer.

He pulled off the highway at the next exit. While he gassed up the RV, she headed inside the small convenience store, stopping to buy coffee at the kiosk by the counter. Returning to the Airstream, she climbed in the driver's side and set her cup in the holder. "I needed a jolt of caffeine to keep me awake. I assumed you wouldn't want any since this is your chance to sleep."

"That's fine," he said.

His response was two words this time. Maybe by the time they got to South Dakota, they'd be communicating in whole sentences again.

But, really, what had she been expecting when she'd steered the conversation into such difficult territory? A heavy sense of regret weighed down on her shoulders as she thought of something she had heard a long time ago. *Forget the mistake. Remember the lesson.*

That advice had proven to be extremely productive in her dealings with issues that cropped up at the hospital. The problem was that she wasn't exactly rational when it came to Steven. If caring for him was a mistake, then what was the lesson? She had loved him once, maybe a lot more than she cared to admit. And it was true that, in the days and months after he left, she had expected him to track her down at some point, if only just to talk and catch up. And when he hadn't, it had hurt her pride. Because, first and foremost, they had been friends. And it would have been fun to talk about his career, her travels, Lilly's wedding and the birth of Polly. Of course, there had been nothing stopping her from reaching out to him. He would have been easy enough to find with the schedule for the bull riding competition as close as a click away.

She hadn't done that, though. Probably pride, once again the logical culprit keeping them apart. The end result was that she and Steven had gone from a situation where they spent almost every day together to zero contact whatsoever. Okay, it was true that once or twice in those first few years, she had allowed herself to google his name to see how he was doing on the circuit, but that was it. And, as time passed, following his accomplishments began to seem slightly stalkerish, and she had forced herself to move on.

Which she had. How successful she had been with that was open to debate. It hadn't been easy. Over the years, she had gone on dates with doctors and men she had met through her coworkers. A lot of them had been nice, but there was no spark. Once or twice, she thought there was potential, but it never seemed to pan out.

She had to assume Steven had continued to date as well, though at present he didn't seem to be in a relationship. That was surprising. She had seen firsthand how beautiful women flocked to the top bull riders. And Steven was the best-looking and the nicest of the lot, at least when she'd known him. She snuck a glance at him in the passenger seat of the trailer. Still as handsome as ever.

That was his problem in a nutshell. He was too perfect. Starting with his idyllic childhood growing up on the ranch, and then, moving on to his success on the rodeo circuit, all the while presenting an image of Mr. No Worries or Cares. His ability to detach himself from stress and worry really was his superpower. She glanced over at him again and his eyes blinked open.

"What?" he asked.

"I didn't say anything," she said.

"Okay," he said.

"Well, I guess I did want to say something. I'm sorry for what I said before about your proposal." She blew out a long sigh. Did eating humble pie really have to be this hard?

"You're allowed to think whatever you want, Etta."

"I know, but I sounded meaner than I intended. It was just so unexpected, that's all. I mean, I had no clue you were going to pop the question, and then to see the two of us on the screen with the whole stadium cheering… well, it threw me for a loop."

"I got that from what you already said," he replied, covering his yawn.

"Sorry. Go back to sleep."

"We can discuss this if you want, but there doesn't seem to be a point to it. Or a whole lot more to say. I asked you to marry me, you said yes. Then you said no, and that was that. I'm really not up for analyzing how it all worked out for the best because we have no way of knowing whether or not that's true."

"Right," she answered instinctively. But then she thought about it. What did that even mean? That breaking up hadn't been the best option?

"I guess we both got what we wanted. I got

to travel and see the country, and you got to be a major star on the PBR circuit, scoring in the top ten at most every event."

His lips bent into a sardonic grin. "I thought you didn't follow my career."

She felt heat spreading up her cheeks, though she was comforted by the fact that it was too dark inside the cab for Steven to see it. "I haven't lately. But I used to check in with the standings once in a while. I was pleased to see that you were doing so well."

"Thanks for that, Etta. And listen. All of this stuff is water under the bridge. I'm just glad I can help you find out what happened to Lilly. And don't waste one moment worrying about my mom or dad giving you the third degree. They're not like that. They've only heard good things about the beautiful nurse I met fifteen years ago while I was in the hospital in Texas. So they're not going to interrogate you about your reasons for not wanting to marry their son."

THIRTEEN

The fifteen-hour drive had taken a decided toll on Steven's leg. Although he had tried to hide his discomfort, Etta noticed his pronounced limp each time they stopped for gas, and she never hesitated to call him out for overextending his time behind the wheel. But he had been adamant about doing his share, and, with two drivers changing off every couple of hours and with a couple of long breaks for all of them to stretch their legs, they made great time getting through Kansas and Nebraska and were well ahead of schedule for a four-o'clock arrival at the ranch.

His parents were waiting on the porch when they pulled into the driveway, his gray-haired dad in his usual plaid shirt and worn jeans and his blonde mother, dressed up for the occasion in a long skirt and cotton blouse tied at the waist. As he drew his mom into a tight hug, Steven said a silent prayer that she'd resist the urge to ask too many questions about his current circumstances. Despite his earlier claim that his mother wouldn't pry, there remained just the tiniest chance she might, if the mood struck, pose a question or two about the reasons for their long-ago breakup. But all his worries dropped away as his folks welcomed their visitors with open arms.

"Etta and Polly," Steven said, stepping back to widen the circle. "These are my parents, Scott and Sandy Hunt. Mom, Dad, this is Etta and her niece, Polly."

"Nice to meet you, Mr. and Mrs. Hunt," Etta said.

"Please. Call us Scott and Sandy," his mom insisted.

"Scott and Sandy, then." Etta smiled. "I want to thank you for letting us hole up here for a bit while we figure things out."

"Wouldn't have it any other way," his dad said. "And we insist that you make yourself at home. We'll hold off on the grand tour for now, but I'm wondering if one of you might know something about horses."

Well done, Dad. Steven was glad he had prepped his father in advance.

There was a moment of silence as all eyes fixed on Polly, whose nod was hardly perceptible.

Scott clapped his hands. "I'm happy to meet a young'un who appreciates beautiful animals. I was just about to head to the barn to check on one of the mares who has been off her feed. I wonder if you'd like to come with me and see how she's doing."

Another small nod of the head, and off Polly went with Scott to the horse barn.

Sandy snaked an arm around Etta's waist and led her into the house. "I'll show you your room, and you can get settled. I put Polly right next door in an adjoining bedroom, but if need be, we can open the trundle bed and she can sleep next to you."

"Thanks, Sandy," Etta said as she followed his mom into the house.

Finding himself alone on the porch, Steven took a moment to breathe in a lungful of clean, fresh air. This truly was God's country, from the rolling hills to the fields of golden grasses. It was home, and he loved it more than any other place on earth. But despite the awesome grandeur of the landscape, he suddenly felt mentally and physically exhausted, a condition he aimed to keep hidden from his mom.

He should have known there was no chance of that.

"You look tired," she said without preamble the moment she returned to the porch. "And I can see that you haven't exactly been following the doctor's orders about avoiding too much stress on your leg."

"Aww, Ma." He shrugged, all of a sudden feeling like a ten-year-old kid allergic to advice. "I really am doing okay."

"I guess I'll have to believe you since you always tell the truth," she said, raising her brow. "In any event. I'm glad we can offer your friends a safe place to stay."

Of course. His mom had an enormous heart for helping others. She hadn't hesitated for even a second when he had called from the road and described their circumstances.

"But," she continued, her eyes sparkling with canny intelligence, "now that you're here, I'm going to stay on you about making good choices. You're not twenty-one anymore, Steven. Serious injuries like yours take longer to heal. Which means you need to listen to what your doctors say."

"Yeah, Ma. I know."

He pulled in another deep breath and resolved not to push back against his mom's unsolicited advice. All of the broken bones and dislocated shoulders he suffered in the ring had been hard on her as well. In fact, it was one of the reasons he had begged her not to visit him fifteen years ago when he ended up in the hospital in Texas. That had been the worst injury of his career, and he knew that it would've caused her untold distress to see him during his recuperation. Talking on the phone was easier. That way, she didn't have to deal with the reality of his bent and bruised body stretched on the bed.

He had often thought that his life was divided between things that had happened before and after he almost lost his life at that rodeo in Dallas. Up until that point in his career, he'd been just muddling along, enjoying the prestige of being part of the circuit. He'd finally become a contender, but he lacked the skills of a true champion. Then two things happened. He got hurt, and Etta rejected his proposal. The fire was in his belly then, and with that new resolve came a determination to be the best. And he'd succeeded beyond his wildest expectations. But that didn't make the risk he took every time he competed any easier on his family.

"I like your Etta," his mom said, pulling him back to the present. "She seems spunky."

He smiled at that, "spunky" being the highest compliment in his mom's vocabulary.

Still, he didn't need her throwing around phrases like "your Etta" and suggesting that the two of them were anything more than friends.

"Remember. We talked about this when I called you yesterday. Etta and I are not in a romantic relationship. I'm just doing what I can to keep her and Polly safe and help solve her sister's murder."

"Of course. It upsets me to think of a little child left without a mom, her dad in jail and her aunt on the run. I was going to say something to Etta when I showed her to her room, but I decided it might be best not to open up old wounds."

"It's not an old wound, Ma. The person who killed Etta's sister is still out there, and Polly won't be safe until he or she is brought to justice. That's why I brought them here, so that they'll be safe while we try to figure out what's going on. I can't begin to tell you how much I appreciate your willingness to offer them a calm haven from all the trouble."

"Your dad and I are glad to help in any way we can." Sandy pushed her hands into the pockets of her faded jeans and tilted her head toward the kitchen. "But right now, since I've exceeded my limit on lecturing, I'm going to go work on dinner. I know I don't need to tell you this, but you and Etta should feel free to use the office as a base of operations. The sooner you get some answers, the better it will be for Polly."

Steven followed his mom into the house and then headed up the stairs.

The guest-room door was open, and he could see that Etta had changed into jeans and a bright yellow T-shirt from their shopping spree at Walmart.

"I like your outfit." He grinned.

"Thanks," she said. She patted her pocket. "I have the thumb drive right here if you're ready to get down to business."

He was, though he wouldn't have minded spending a few more minutes admiring Etta's relaxed style.

He led the way down the stairs and along the first-floor hallway into the office. "I'll use my dad's tablet and see what I can dig up about the law firm representing Greg. You can use my mom's desk by the window. I assume her password is still John 3:16. She chose her favorite Bible verse so she won't forget."

Etta settled back into Sandy's ergonomic chair. "Wow, this is supercomfortable. I could work here forever." She tapped in the pass code and slipped the USB into the port.

"Let's hope that won't be necessary, though I have to admit to being intrigued at the thought of you and Polly staying here until she enters college. Would that be South Dakota State?" Steven smirked as he took a seat on the couch. Etta had been teasing when she made that suggestion, but he did wonder what she thought about his home state.

Tablet open, he began a search for information about the law firm of Thompson, Colfax and Bickler. There was a definite connection there, he was sure of it, but progress was slow going, as he waded through pages after page of laudatory claims, searching for a connection between Lilly and Matt Bickler.

He wondered if Etta was having some degree of success. Her eyes remained fixed on the screen.

A loud sigh followed by an exclamation of delight drew him across the room to join her.

"Look at this, Steven!" Her eyes shone with excitement as she pointed to the screen. "It's an old *People* magazine article about a group of radical college students from the seventies. They were known as the JIF8, or Justice in Full, and they were famous for using violence to advance their political agenda. They'd plant bombs at big events like parades and concerts. Dozens of people were hurt, and a handful died after one particular explosion at a soccer match in downtown Detroit."

"Serious stuff then," Steven said, leaning in for a closer look.

"So serious that the FBI eventually raided their headquarters, and seven of the eight original members were arrested, tried and sent to jail. But one member of the group, the actual bomb maker, managed to evade the authorities. Her name was Belinda Lee Caruso. And look at this! Lilly circled her picture on the thumb drive." She pulled up a photo of a twenty-year old woman, with wire-rimmed glasses and long hair pulled into a long, flowing braid. "Could she be the focus of the big score Lilly mentioned to Jordan Shapiro?"

Etta could barely contain her excitement as she settled back in the chair. "I'm trying to stay calm here, but this has to be a major clue, doesn't it?" She scrolled through a couple more pages until she came upon a letter to an agent, asking if there was any interest in a work of nonfiction about a seventies fugitive who had been hiding in plain sight. "And check this out! Lilly obviously felt confident enough to shop this idea around."

Steven's eyes narrowed as he took a moment to read what Etta had pulled up on the screen. "We seem to be getting ahead of ourselves here. Who's to say Lilly had either the evidence or the writing chops to get a deal from a publisher?"

But Steven's less-than-enthusiastic reaction failed to dampen Etta's eagerness. "Don't forget. Lilly was a reporter, so she wouldn't have gone chasing a story without securing the necessary proof. There could be information that she didn't load on the thumb drive."

He nodded. "True. And it's easy to imagine that Belinda Caruso wouldn't want to draw any attention from the FBI."

"I know, right." They were on to something. She knew it.

It seemed that Steven did, too, because he appeared more interested by the minute. "So, presumably, Lilly showed her hand while she was snooping around, and Belinda Caruso realized what she was up to."

An overwhelming feeling of sadness suddenly swamped Etta's senses. She could readily imagine her sister's excitement as she uncovered such a big scoop. Lilly had always been prone to jump in with both feet without recognizing the consequences. In her zeal, she might have gotten careless. And that was a fatal mistake.

"But even if we accept the fact that Belinda killed Lilly," Steven said, his voice interrupting her melancholy musing, "who are these men after Polly?"

That was the question. They had already zeroed in on the connection to the law firm, and there were other names and descriptions they had picked up along the way—like the man named TJ. But how did a radical fugitive from the seventies fit into the equation?

Steven pulled out his phone. "It's after five. Polly and my dad are probably back from the barn, which means that, any minute, my mom is going to be calling us for dinner."

Right on cue, Sandy Hunt's voice boomed out through the hall.

"Steven! Etta! Time for supper."

Steven grinned. "Ha! I told you. I don't know how it happens, but whenever I come home, my stomach resets to mom time."

The copies could wait, Etta decided. She followed Steven out of the office and into the dining room. Polly was already seated at the table, her smile hinting that she had enjoyed her time in the barn.

Steven counted aloud the places around the table. "Six?" He raised an eyebrow in his mother's direction.

"Seb's on his own tonight since Tacy has Bible study. He'll join us after work."

"Seb, huh?" Etta tucked in a secret smile. Since meeting Steven, she had been intrigued by the existence of his identical twin brother. "We're alike only in appearance," Steven had told her once with a mysterious wink. Perhaps tonight she'd find out what that meant.

Funny, though. When Seb ambled into the dining room midway through dinner, it was the twins' current physical differences that most surprised her.

Seb was broad and burly, so different than Steven's wiry physique. Then again, it might have been the uniform—the gray shirt tucked into creased black pants and the felted cowboy hat he quickly removed from his head—that made him appear taller and a lot more formidable.

"Nice hairstyle, little brother," Seb declared. Steven smiled, stood up and then allowed himself to be pulled into a tight bear hug by his brother. "And who are these beautiful ladies joining us for dinner?"

Steven was quick to make the introductions, though it seemed clear from the twinkle in his brother's eye that Seb already knew who they were. "Etta, Polly, you probably guessed that this is my brother, Seb. But you should call him Sebastian."

"Hey, hey, hey. Let's not go there. Otherwise, I might have to retaliate by mocking your new look."

"Boys! Enough!" Sandy's no-nonsense tone put an end to the good-natured bickering, and Seb slid into the open chair next to his brother.

"Say, Ma. I wouldn't say no to some of your famous roast beef."

Surreptitiously observing Seb from across the table, Etta began to revise her original assessment. She could see that while there were a number of differences in Seb and Steven's outward appearances, both men shared the same strong jaw, dark, intelligent eyes and crooked smile that made it obvious they were brothers.

"So," Seb said once the last piece of pie had disappeared from the dish. "I have some information that might be of interest."

Sandy picked up the cue and made a move to shepherd Polly from the table. "If you don't mind helping me load the dishwasher," she said to the little girl, "I'll tell you a story about that mare you met today in the barn and how she led Seb on a mighty chase for three miles into town."

When the kitchen door swung closed behind them, the mood of the dining room changed. Gone was the carefree atmosphere of the past hour, leaving in its place a mood of worried anticipation. Seb didn't waste any time getting to the gist of it.

"Dad started filling me in about what's going on with Etta. Which is interesting, since earlier today one of my deputies took a call from the desk clerk at the Bluebird Hotel. Apparently, a man checking in was asking about a woman and a little girl staying at the Hunt family ranch. The clerk was suspicious, especially after he caught sight of a fairly large handgun tucked in the waistband of the stranger's pants." Seb paused to rub a hand across his chin and then directed his words to his twin brother. "So I'm thinking that maybe this would be a good time for you to tell me the rest of the story."

FOURTEEN

"Where to start?" Steven mused, holding Etta's eyes. He shook his head.

"How about the beginning?" his brother suggested.

Easier said than done. Etta had killed a man in self-defense, not a crime in and of itself. But the leaving-the-scene part...that was different. Could he describe the situation without mentioning several of the salient facts?

"How much did Dad tell you about why we're here?"

Seb shrugged. "Not much. He said that you had gone to Texas to see a woman he described as the one who got away." He glanced at Etta, who shifted in her seat.

"Not sure why he said that, but whatever."

"He said that her sister had been murdered. I assume he was talking about you, Etta." He faced her again. "I'm sorry for your loss.

And that's about it. I assume there's a lot he left out."

Steven sighed. "Well, the fact that this guy has turned up in town, asking questions, changes the dynamic. Polly's in danger because of something she might have seen or heard the day her mom was killed, and she hasn't been able to tell us what that is."

"Complicated." Seb shook his head.

"That's an understatement." Steven looked across the table at Etta. She had remained mum during the discussion, allowing him to decide how much to say. When neither of them spoke, Seb continued.

"Well, so far, the guy at the motel is just sniffing around. It seems likely that no one outside the family knows that Etta and Polly are here, and we can do our best to keep it that way. But just in case, I can have one of my deputies keep an eye on the motel and make sure there are no other unexpected visitors."

Steven exhaled a long sigh of relief. No matter how dire the circumstances, his family would always have his back. But that worked both ways. He needed to get Seb up to speed about what he might be getting into.

"All cards on the table here, bro. Back in Texas, Etta used deadly force to defend herself when a man broke into her house and came for Polly. I know you won't approve, but we left the scene rather than reporting what had happened to the authorities. The original plan was to head for the ranch after a few quick stops to see what we could find out about what was going on. I thought I'd been able to stay off the radar, but given the number of cameras everywhere, it was probably just a matter of time before they sussed out my identity." And once they figured out who he was, it wouldn't have taken them long to figure out about his family's ranch and where they may be headed next.

Seb nodded. "I know I'm not telling you anything you haven't figured out already, but this seems a lot bigger than just a murder. First thing you learn as a cop or an investigator—follow the money. Someone is bankrolling this operation for reasons that at this point aren't completely clear."

Etta pulled in a short intake of breath, and both men turned to face her.

"Wow," she said. "It just suddenly hit me to hear it all broken down that way."

"I get it," Seb said. "But I take it you've made some progress in identifying your sister's killer."

"We think so," Etta agreed. She explained what they'd found on Lilly's USB. "It's just an assumption at this point, but we think Lilly discovered Belinda Lee Caruso living somewhere in Texas. Again, we're guessing here, but we think this woman got wind of what Lilly was up to and killed her to keep her secret from being exposed. That's our theory, anyway. At this point we don't have any evidence."

Seb pushed back his chair and stood up. "Okay, then. I'm thinking I should head over to the Bluebird and maybe see if our inquisitive visitor is still on his own or if anyone else has joined him."

"I'd like to come with you," Steven said.

"No." Seb shook his head. "It's best to keep things as low-key as possible. I'll just stroll by the office and look for a chance to ask a few questions. In the meantime, you two should dig up what you can about anyone and everyone who could be involved with this fugitive. Maybe her coconspirators? Most of them may have served their time and gotten out of jail. It's hard to understand why they'd be helping her since she was the one who escaped punishment, but you never know."

After Seb left, Etta took Polly upstairs to

put her to bed. Steven returned to the office to check into the whereabouts of the other seven members of the JIF8. But that task was proving to be nearly impossible without access to a larger database. After an hour of searching, all he knew for certain was that three of Belinda Caruso's colleagues had died in prison and the other four had served their time and eventually been released from jail.

On a whim, he opened his billfold and pulled out the license he had been using to support his identity as Matt Bickler, along with that blue-and-white sticker. It read, "Reelect TJ Bishop for Texas AG."

TJ. Wasn't that the name Etta had heard mentioned by one of the men who'd broken into the house? A quick search of the website of the current attorney general revealed that he was a former partner at the law firm of Thompson, Colfax and Bickler.

"The plot thickens," he muttered to himself.

The office door opened, and Etta walked over to join him.

"Did you find anything?" she asked.

"Still working on it." He looked up at her. She was looking especially pretty with her cute new haircut and her eyes so bright with anticipation. "Polly go down all right?"

"Yup. I tried to see if she had any reaction to the name Belinda Caruso, but I didn't notice any change in her countenance. She just seemed tired. And happy. Even after just a few hours spent with your dad in the horse barn, the change in her is amazing. Your parents are both so kind."

Well, she wasn't going to get any argument there.

Etta smiled and Steven's heart began to beat harder in his chest. How had his dad described her—the one who got away? He supposed that was more than a little true as he had been slowly coming to terms with the real reason he had gone to Texas just a few days ago.

Maybe he should share that thought with Etta. He glanced at her and held her gaze. "You know all that personal stuff we discussed during the drive here from Texas? I feel like we opened up some cold, hard truths about our relationship. But I realized that I really do need to apologize for my proposal. I don't know what I was thinking, arranging to have it shown on the jumbotron, but I do remember praying that you'd say yes."

Etta smiled again. "Well, in a way, it was successful, since that's what happened. But as long as we're clearing the air, I'm sorry, too. I shouldn't have hijacked the conversation so long about past grievances. My only excuse is that my adrenaline was still pumping after you rescued me at the house. And…" She shrugged. "I do tend to get caught up with ideas that get stuck in my head. But before I forget, I thought of something important when I was tucking Polly into bed. Remember when all of this started, and we were looking for Polly at the house?"

Steven nodded. Apparently, now wasn't the time to admit his real reason for his visit to Texas.

Etta continued. "When I went outside to see if Polly was in the yard, I ran into a neighbor who was taking pictures for the neighborhood-share app. And I had a thought. It's probably unlikely, but maybe if we went to the site, we could find a photo of someone who resembles Belinda Caruso."

"On it," he said. It only took a couple of minutes for him to pull up the app and then a few more to find the photos from the block party. "What do you think of her as a possibility?" He pointed to a picture of a tall, slender woman in a plaid sundress.

"I don't think so," Etta said, shaking her

head. "Why don't I print the photo in the article, and we can see if we can look for similarities?"

A few minutes later, she returned to Steven's side with a grainy photo of a young Belinda Caruso. Lilly had circled the photo and written a question in the margin.

Birthmark?

"Do you have a magnifying glass?" she asked Steven.

He handed her one from the drawer, and she held it over the picture. Yup. Lilly was right. There was a small diamond-shaped birthmark on Belinda's neck.

She tacked the photo to the bulletin board above the desk as Steven scrolled through what seemed to be an endless file of block-party photos.

A shuffling sound outside the office caught their attention, and Etta walked across the room and opened the door. There stood Polly, her thumb in her mouth and her fingers wrapped around the bunny she was clutching to her chest.

"You okay, hon?" Etta asked.

Polly nodded.

"Can't sleep, huh? That's okay. I'm almost ready for bed myself."

Polly's eyes widened and her hand started to shake as her trembling finger pointed toward the photo frozen on the computer screen. On either side of the picture were kids holding Super Soakers, and in the center were a half-dozen adults caught in the crossfire, all with dripping-wet hair and sodden clothing. At the back of the group, barely discernable at first glance, was Lynn Weber. Lilly and Greg's next-door neighbor…and clearly the source of Polly's distress.

Two hours later, Etta was still wide-awake as the implications of their recent discovery played through her head.

She would have never suspected that Lilly's kindly neighbor was a wanted fugitive who had evaded the police for years. Even as she recognized the terror in her niece's eyes at Lynn's picture, it was still hard to imagine the gray-haired woman who wore a smile every morning as she walked her golden retriever down the block as a ruthless killer. A bomb maker with no respect for human life.

But once she had settled a greatly agitated Polly back into bed, she and Steven had compared the two photos side by side, they were able to notice some similarities. Lynn Weber and Belinda Caruso both had high cheek-bones and sloped shoulders, but that was hardly enough to claim a definite match. Especially since there were plenty of differences as well, including eye color—"contacts," as Lilly had suggested—hair color and cut. Etta had pointed to her own red hair—"Almost too easy," she'd said. Unlike Lynn, Belinda had a pointy chin and thin lips, but those could have been changed or disguised with makeup or plastic surgery. The truth was that if hadn't been for Polly's reaction to the photo of her neighbor, Etta and Steven might never have made the connection.

Despite all the points of dispute, there was one key factor that convinced Etta and Steven that they had found Belinda Caruso's alter ego. In the block-party photo, Lynn's hair was wet and limp, having been doused with spray from the water guns. It was so limp, in fact, that it fell short of her neck and allowed for an excellent view of a diamond-shaped birthmark identical to Belinda Caruso's.

Had Lilly noticed that birthmark when she'd watched Lynn swimming in her back-yard pool? Or was there something else that had caused her sister to realize that her neighbor bore a distinct resemblance to the seventies fugitive? Leave it to Lilly. How many other residents of Silver Creek remembered or, for that matter, ever knew the story about the JIF8 and the bomb-maker fugitive?

Etta sure hadn't. But now that she thought about it, other clues to Lynn's deception had been there all along. Like the unlikely coincidence of her neighbor showing up on the doorstep immediately after the break-in. And hadn't Greg told Steven that a neighbor had advised him to hire Sam Colfax to represent him in the case? What better way to subtly undermine Greg's defense.

Anger threaded through Etta's senses as she thought about what could have happened the day her sister was killed. The police who arrived at the murder scene had been quick to decide that it was a domestic dispute turned deadly, but her brother-in-law never wavered in his claim that his wife was alive when he left for work. No one suspected that a kindly neighbor might have dropped by the house that morning and waited until Lilly wasn't looking before slipping poison into the carafe and her mug.

It would have been almost too easy, casting Greg into the role of the convenient scapegoat. But there was only one snag in that plan, and that was Polly.

Where was her little niece when all of that was going on? What had she heard, and what had she seen? The answers remained locked up inside of her. Maybe someday they'd find out the truth.

Around midnight, Etta finally drifted off to sleep. When she finally woke up, sunlight was already streaming through the window, and there was a message from Steven on her burner phone.

Decided to show Seb the photos of the SUV that followed us in Silver Creek. The driver with the moustache is definitely one of the staffers working for the Texas AG. More grist for the mill, right?

Etta sat up in bed as a sense of guilt pulsed through her. She'd been asleep while Steven had been working, following through on the information they'd discovered the night before.

Next to her on the trundle bed, Polly was waking up. Her tiny fingers reached out to squeeze Etta's hand, and Etta held on tight as she twisted around on her side for a better view of her little niece.

"You doing okay, Pol?" she asked, blinking back a tear.

The little girl's nod was slow and certain.

"Good. Now what do you say to heading downstairs to get something to eat?"

Breakfast was a feast of scrambled eggs and bacon, oatmeal and toast. Seb and Steven were still out, but as she and Polly ate, Scott filled in her niece on his plans for the day. "Any chance you'd like to join me when I check on the horses?" he asked, his eyes twinkling as he took in the little girl's delight. Five minutes later, they were out the door and headed for the stables.

"And then there were two," Sandy said with a smile. "What can I do to help you get settled in this morning? Really, Etta. Having you here is lovely. And Steven seems happier than he's been in a long time. And that's a wonderful gift for a mother's heart."

Etta's eyes went misty. After all the drama of the past few days, Sandy's kindness had somehow produced a wave of unexpected tears. She quickly turned her head to hide the wetness on her face.

"Would you mind if I did a wash?"

"Of course," Sandy said. "Come with me downstairs and I'll help you get started. If you have time, you may want to hang your stuff on the line. It's more work, but you can't beat that fresh scent."

Sandy was right, Etta decided a half hour later as she carried a load of T-shirts and jeans to the back of the ranch house. The morning sun warmed her shoulders as she pinned her clothes on the line. The air was fresh, and the landscape was breathtaking. No wonder Steven loved it here. Maybe if things had been different, she might have come to feel the same way.

She banished those thoughts with a shake of her head. She'd had her chance with Steven. And she had rejected his proposal and sent him on his way. So why was she focused on all of this now?

Perhaps it was the thoughtful way he had treated her and Polly. And others as well. Watching him talk to his parents and joke with Seb in such a fond way. Even the way he interacted with Kenny, the kid from the trailer park, who had seemed over the moon to receive the gift of a signed cowboy hat.

But Steven had always been kind. So what exactly explained her sudden change of heart? All along, had she been secretly hoping for a second chance? Was it even possible for their love story to have a different ending?

Maybe. But only if she put aside her stubborn pride and allowed herself to trust him again with her heart.

A sudden cool breeze from the west sent a shiver up her arms. She looked up and noticed that a few dark clouds had drifted across the now overcast sky. Her gaze flitted toward the still-wet clothes she had fixed to the line. If she didn't know better, she'd think that it was about to rain. But hadn't the sun been shining just minutes before?

She received her first lesson in the vagaries of South Dakota weather as the first drops landed on her head. What to do next? Should she pull down the clothing she'd just pinned up or rush to seek shelter inside the house?

The choice was made for her as the sky darkened even more and rain began to fall in thick sheets. As thunder rumbled, and a crack of lightning split the air, she began to run, abandoning the clothes on the line.

"Sandy?" she called out, rushing into the house and through the hall.

No answer, just the thudding of boots against the kitchen floor.

"Sandy?" she cried out a second time.

"I'm upstairs, hon. Be there in a second."

Two things happened, almost at once. A

man bounded out of the kitchen, sprinting toward the front door, and Sandy appeared at the opposite end of the hallway, her head bent over a stack of folded sheets she was holding.

Etta opened her mouth, but she couldn't get out any words.

The front door slammed shut, and Sandy set down the sheets, looking concerned when she noticed Etta. "Oh, honey. Are you all right?"

Etta pressed against the older woman's shoulder, her face wet with tears. "You didn't see him?" she choked out.

Sandy's brow creased. "See who?"

"I was hanging clothes when it started to rain. But when I came inside... I heard someone in the kitchen. I thought it was you, but it was a man."

Sandy slipped her phone from the pocket of her apron and punched in a number. "Scott? We've had an intruder. Call Seb and Steven and tell them to get up here as fast as they can." As she talked, she grabbed a set of keys from the counter and walked across the room. It only took her a second to unlock the gun cabinet and insert a magazine into a formidable-looking pistol.

She pulled up a chair and faced the back door.

"Now, we wait." She remained in position until her husband and two sons had arrived at the ranch house. Only then did she eject the magazine from the pistol and lock it back in the cabinet.

"There's no trace of him. He's gone," Steven said after they'd searched the property. He sat down next to her at the kitchen table, and the others followed suit.

"Where's Polly?" Etta asked.

"I called my wife Tacy and she came over to get her. Our place is right next door," Seb assured her. "Take your time and describe what happened before and after you saw the intruder."

She was relieved to hear Polly was safe. "It's not much of a story," Etta admitted, but she explained what happened.

"Do you have a description?" Seb queried. "Tall? Short? Young? Old?"

Etta shook her head. "It all happened so fast. I'm sorry."

"No worries." Steven met and held her anxious glance. "I just wonder what he was doing inside the house. Was he looking for Polly and thought he might find her at the ranch?"

"Could be," Seb agreed. "Once we're through here, I'll head into the office and arrange for a couple of deputies to provide round-the-clock protection."

Steven pulled out his phone and scrolled down to a photo of a well-dressed man in a three-piece suit. He handed his cell to Etta. "Thought you might be interested in something I found this morning. The man in the picture is Terrance Joseph Bishop, also known as TJ, current attorney general for the state of Texas. Also, coincidentally, a former partner in the law firm of Thompson, Colfax and Bickler. Recognize the woman standing next to him?"

"Is that…?" She looked up at Steven. "Lynn Weber…aka Belinda Caruso?"

"Yup. She's wearing glasses and her hair's different, but I'm pretty sure that's our little terrorist, standing next to her son."

"Her son?" Etta gasped.

"Yeah." Steven nodded. "This is getting really complicated. But it gets us closer to figuring things out."

"Can I see that, too?" As Seb reached for the phone, his gaze moved past Etta toward the back door. He stood up and paced across the room, moving slowly and taking his time dragging his fingers under the counters and below the cabinets along the wall. He stopped suddenly in front of a lamp and then tilted the base sideways to reveal a small button-shaped device affixed to the shade.

Then he raised his fingers to his lips and motioned that they should follow him outside.

FIFTEEN

"A bug!" Etta exclaimed. "That means they can listen to our private conversations. How can we ever feel safe?"

Sandy reached over and took her hand. "Don't fret, hon. Seb's the sheriff. If they come after you or Polly, he'll bring the force of the law down on their heads."

Etta nodded. She believed Seb—and Steven—would do everything possible to protect them.

Steven blew out a long sigh. "That's all true, Ma, but we've got to stop playing defense on this. We need to do something proactive, like lure Lynn to the ranch. With no evidence to link her to Lilly's murder, it could be our only chance of getting a confession."

It seemed a bit reckless—classic Steven—but he had a point. She was tired of running.

She wanted to know what had happened to her sister.

"Would she be willing to come here?" Seb asked.

Steven shrugged. "Maybe she'd do it if she knew that we have evidence linking her to JIF8 and Belinda Caruso. That's our best bargaining chip to get her attention."

"But is the evidence all that solid? From what you told me, it's just a picture and article from an old magazine," Seb said.

"True," Steven admitted. "But I can't imagine Lynn would be pleased to have it out there. And, not only that, but we have the connection between the men who have been pursuing us and the office of the current AG. I assume Lynn has a stake in her son's political future. And with TJ Bishop currently in a tight race for reelection, neither of them would want even a whiff of scandal."

"Okay. Let's say she agrees to come to the ranch. What's the endgame? What can Etta ask for in trade for her silence?" Sandy asked.

Etta was quick to answer. "Polly's safety—guaranteed. That would be my main demand."

"But how could you trust a terrorist to keep to her part of the bargain?" Scott asked.

Steven shook his head. "We're getting too deep in the weeds here. There isn't actually going to be any sort of trade. We're just dangling the idea as a way to convince Lynn that we mean business."

"Hmm." Seb's lips twisted in a sly smile. "And this is where the listening device fits in. They don't know we found it, so we use it to our advantage."

"Lull them into a false sense of security," Steven declared.

"Right," Seb agreed. "If Etta can talk Lynn into coming to South Dakota, we use a wire in the hope of extracting a confession."

But first, they needed to head inside so Etta could call Lynn and issue the invitation. Etta's fingers shook as she tapped in the numbers to make the call.

"Hello." The sound of Lynn's voice sent shivers up Etta's spine, but she took a deep breath and forced herself to speak.

"Lynn, this is Etta Mitchell, Lilly Sanderson's sister. I'm staying at a friend's ranch in South Dakota, and I was hoping to persuade you to join me here."

"Now, why would I want to do that?" Lynn asked—she seemed to be feigning confusion.

Etta pulled in another deep breath and

made a concerted effort to moderate her tone. This would be a lot harder if Lynn agreed to come for a visit, so she needed to get used to remaining calm under pressure.

"Because I know who you are…and I know what you did. But what I want is simple. You need to call off your lackeys and leave us alone. In return, I'll stay mum about what I know about Belinda Caruso and hand over what evidence I have. But we have to meet face-to-face, just you and me, and it has to be here in South Dakota."

There was a pause on the line. "Why can't we talk in Texas?"

Etta didn't answer.

"Cat got your tongue, eh? Seems like you're the one with all the secrets and lies. I suppose you may have some explaining to do about the body that was discovered on Dogwood Drive. Or about the fact that your fingerprints were all over the murder weapon," she said smoothly. "Really, Etta? Hitting someone in the head with a frying pan? How positively domestic of you. And here I was thinking that nurses are trained to save lives."

Deep breaths. Deep breaths. "I can explain my actions, Lynn. But can you? My sister dug up some very convincing evidence linking you to JIF8. If anything happens to me or to Polly, I've made arrangements for everything to be sent to the FBI. I assume they'll be very interested in learning about your double life. And so will the reporters covering your son's campaign." She paused for a moment to let that sink in. "Shall I text you the address and plan on seeing you tomorrow?"

Lynn caved, as they'd hoped, and agreed to come to South Dakota. "Just the two of us women for a little exchange," Etta said as she wrapped up the call. But she had no expectation that would be the case.

She didn't think she'd to be able to settle down that night when she went to bed. But the sight of her little niece, curled up in the trundle bed with her bunny, reminded her that nothing had changed since Greg had been handcuffed and taken to jail. She had been charged with the duty of keeping Polly safe, and that was what she was going to do. It was that thought that allowed her to drift off to sleep.

The buzz of a text jolted her awake. Daylight was streaming into the room. Bleary-eyed, she read the message that Lynn's flight was on schedule to arrive at twelve o'clock sharp. Her eyes flashed down to the time on her phone—7:00 a.m.—which meant she had only five hours to get ready for the meeting.

Treading lightly down the stairs, she poked her head into the kitchen. Steven was already awake, a stack of pancakes and a few sausages on the plate in front of him. He stood up to greet her with a smile.

"Morning," she said.

Her voice must have quavered because Steven walked over to where she was standing and pulled her in close. "You still hanging in there?"

She nodded, suddenly teary.

"You know you're wonderful, right?" He looked down at her with his warm, dark eyes, his arm still around her shoulders. "Smart and courageous and kind and..."

A blush of warmth bloomed on her cheeks. "Steven, no. I'm not any of those things. The truth is that I..."

He released her suddenly and pointed to the listening device on the lamp.

Message received. Anything said in this room would be heard by the person who had planted the bug.

This wasn't the time for emotional revelations. She had always known that the trip north might mark the beginning of the end of their relationship, that being home would cause Steven to yearn for a return to normal. And who could blame him? His actual life was pretty great—the ranch and the horses and the loving family who were always there to support him and welcome him home. Nothing remotely similar to what it had been like for her growing up, with an absent mother and a delinquent sister.

But for all her faults, Lilly had come to understand that she was worthy as a child of God, while Etta was the one who'd refused to change. She continued stubbornly pushing people away—Steven, her colleagues on the job, even Lilly, in the end. A wave of regret washed over her. How had she let this happen? Not only had she allowed a chasm to form between herself and her only sister, but she had also forfeited time they could have spent together, time she could never replace. Maybe she didn't deserve happiness. Clearly, she hadn't tried hard enough to be a sister, a fiancée, or a friend.

She pulled herself out of her funk and looked at Steven. He held her gaze and pointed to the door, then gestured that she should follow him outside.

Once they reached the lawn, he put an arm

around her shoulders and pulled her close. "You looked worried. And who can blame you? This is going to be a hard day for you more than the rest of us. I realized this morning that there's one major disadvantage to being home that I hadn't anticipated. It's the fact that we haven't had much of a chance to talk."

She forced a smile. "It has been a big change to have so many people around all the time. Especially after we spent so long on the road, doing almost everything together, with very little time apart."

"You make it sound like that was a bad thing."

He raised an eyebrow, and her heart did a somersault in her chest. Maybe she had been wrong in her previous imaginings. Steven did not view their trip to the ranch as an end of their relationship. It seemed possible—dare she hope?—that he saw it as a kind of beginning.

"I didn't say it was a bad thing," she spluttered, all of a sudden nervous about the emotions crashing around in her brain. "I like hanging out with you. Even if it means that we're stuck in a car or a van or even in the Airstream."

"Good," he said. He reached for her hand and brought it to his lips. "I feel the same way. I didn't realize it at first, but that was what I was hoping for when I showed up on your doorstep in Silver Creek. Not the part about the men following after us and trying to hurt you and kidnap Polly, of course. But, as for spending so much time together, yeah, I liked that a lot."

The rest of the morning passed in a blur. Once Steven finished his breakfast, he showed her where Seb's team had set up a wire to record her conversation with Lynn. Then Seb himself arrived with a report that so far, all was proceeding according to plan. Lynn's plane had landed right on schedule at the Rapid City Regional Airport, and she had rented a car for the drive to the ranch.

"Is she traveling alone?" Etta asked.

Seb shook his head. "Not a chance. Separate cars. Got to keep up the pretense that she's here on her own. But we're expecting company. Don't worry about that."

An hour later, the rumble of tires along the driveway heralded the arrival of a visitor. Etta was watching through the window as a blue Mercedes SUV pulled into a space at the end of the drive. The driver's side door opened, and Lynn stepped out.

Go time.

Etta pulled in a breath and waited. She was as ready as she'd ever be. *Help me, Lord*, she pleaded in a whispered prayer. *Guide my words and rule my actions.* Then she closed her eyes and counted to five before she answered the knock at the door.

Short and wiry, with her midlength gray bob and oversize glasses, Lynn Weber looked just as Etta remembered. Then again, why would she have changed since the last time Etta had seen her, standing at her front door in Silver Creek with a plate of cookies?

Hmm. She had almost forgotten about those cookies. Good thing they had left them behind in the rush out the door. Given everything they now knew about Lynn, she wouldn't have been surprised if there had been some unusual ingredient included in the recipe.

"Hello, Etta." Lynn's artificial smile quickly faded from her lips. "I see that you changed your do. It looks nice. Different, but very stylish."

Etta instinctively ran her fingers through her cropped hair. "I thought we could talk outside on the patio."

She led the way down the hall and through the kitchen, then out the back door.

"Lovely home your friends have here," Lynn said.

Once again, Etta didn't acknowledge the compliment. As Lynn bent to admire the yellow-and-purple pansies on the patio. Etta's hand went to the listening device taped to her chest. Although it seemed unlikely that Lynn would bare her soul and confess to crimes old and new, Seb thought it was best to be prepared just in case. Whenever his team had the chance to act on an arrest, they'd take it.

Etta took a seat at the round patio table, motioning to Lynn that she should do the same. She had decided in advance not to offer refreshments. Why pretend this little get-together was something it wasn't?

"First, I want to thank you for coming here today. We do need to talk, and this didn't seem like a conversation we could have on the phone. What I am asking for is simple. I want your assurance that Polly will be safe. In return, I agree to destroy the evidence on Lilly's thumb drive connecting you to Belinda Caruso."

Lynn opened her mouth to respond, but Etta shut down whatever she intended to say.

"There's nothing you can say that will change the facts. My sister was an astute observer of people. And in the course of living next door to you, she somehow discovered your real identity. I'm not sure how you found out what she was working on, but once you did, you realized that she had enough information to blow your cover. So you killed her. Simple as that."

Lynn blew a short breath through her nose and shook her head.

"Dear, sweet, naive Etta. I think you've fixed on me as a convenient scapegoat to help you deal with to the loss of your sister. I'm sorry Lilly was killed. She was a nice person and a good neighbor, but you know as well as I do that she could be headstrong and willful, especially when she didn't get her way. I can't count the times that I heard her arguing with Greg on the patio or yelling at Polly for wandering into the yard."

Etta felt her whole body tense. "Lilly loved her family."

Lynn shrugged. "I'm glad you believe that, but she certainly had an odd way of showing it. And it's certainly your right to ignore the facts if it helps you cope."

A surge of anger pulsed through Etta's

veins. She wanted to reach across the table and slap Lynn. But this was exactly the type of thing she had resolved to avoid. She looked down at her watch and checked the time. Twelve fifteen. It wouldn't be long now. She just needed to be patient in allowing Lynn to control the narrative.

Steven's heart drummed a staccato beat in his chest. Was it going to work? The plan had made sense when they had discussed it last night. But now, in the cold light of day, there seemed to be way too many variables at play.

A cold bead of sweat trickled down his back.

He hated leaving Etta at the house with Lynn. But this was the only way. And Seb had assured him that his men were watching the homestead. But still.

He'd never forgive himself if anything happened to Etta.

It had been dawning on him little by little over the last few days that she was a great deal more than just a friend. Obviously, she was beautiful, and time had only made her face softer and kinder. But her looks had never been the only attraction. He had discovered early on that she was made of deeper stuff.

Etta had accused him of trying to rescue her, of thinking that he could solve all her problems by whisking her away from her dysfunctional sister and into the bosom of his own traditional family. Well, maybe she'd had a point. He had imagined himself as a sort of knight in shining armor, offering his love and security. But what he'd viewed as romantic motivation, she seemed to have judged as some sort of misplaced machismo.

Hopefully, he and Etta had put all that behind them. It had taken a while, but they seemed to have landed in a pretty good place. Especially after their talk that morning. He hadn't realized what a toll all the planning and anticipation was taking on Etta. She had placed her life on hold to protect Polly, and circumstances had catapulted her into a hornet's nest of drama, danger and intrigue. But she had risen to the challenge. Through it all she had never once allowed herself to give up.

He still believed he and Etta should have been able to make it work. And he suspected that she felt the same way, too. He had seen the look in her eyes when they were standing outside on the patio. Maybe their timing hadn't been right fifteen years ago. Maybe he hadn't fought for her hard enough. It didn't matter. That was in the past. It was the future that he cared about now. And he wanted a future that included Etta. He loved her. He'd always loved her. Tomorrow, when all of this was over, he was going to tell her how he felt. And if she tried to walk away again, well, this time, he wouldn't let pride get in his way. He'd just follow her back to Texas.

But first, they had to deal with Lynn and her minions. Impatience threaded through his limbs. The hay was tickling his nose where he was lying crouched in the loft, and his leg twinged from inactivity. He felt a strong desire to crack his knuckles. Anything to keep his mind off the waiting.

But they were as ready as they would ever be for what would happen next.

He glanced down at the scene below him in the hayloft. Cameras and listening devices had been installed out of sight on the beams around the stable. And there was his father looking completely at ease as he groomed Sandstorm, his favorite horse, and chatted with the little girl standing by his side. Steven took a deep breath and tried to stem his growing anxiety. This was crazy. He was usually the reckless one. But this involved Etta and his family and Polly. And there was no denying the level of risk. He closed his eyes and offered a silent prayer. *Please, God. Grant Your protection and wisdom.* The tenseness around his shoulders eased a bit, but his heart continued to thud.

He opened his eyes as the crunch of gravel announced the arrival of an approaching vehicle. This was it then, the moment they had been waiting for. His mind registered the sunlight penetrating the gloomy space as the barn door slowly slid open and the hinges made a creaking sound, followed by the thudding of footsteps against the wood plank floor. He could see his father's back stiffen as he slowly turned around. Three men stood framed by the open doorway, each holding a pistol.

Steven clenched his fingers. He wished he had a weapon. But Seb had only agreed that he could come along if he promised to stay out of the action, claiming he was too much a liability as a civilian, and an injured one at that. In truth, he suspected that his brother had allowed him a place in the hayloft to keep him as far away from Etta as he possibly could.

"Who are you? And what do you want?" his dad asked the strangers.

"Never mind who we are. We're here for the girl."

"And you think I'm just going to let you take her?" Scott sneered.

"Actually, we do. We can be pretty persuasive."

His father reached for a short plank, which had been propped against the stall. "So can I. You're not going to shoot me in my own barn. Why don't you put those guns away, and we can talk?"

Scott Hunt had been instructed to draw out the conversation as long as possible. But knowing what the plan was and watching it play out were two totally different things.

One of the men chuckled. Steven realized with a start that it was Matt Bickler.

"Look. We don't want any trouble. We won't touch the aunt. But we need the kid." He waved his gun toward the girl. She hadn't turned around, but his father had thrown a protective arm on her shoulder.

"Look," Scott continued, "my son is the sheriff. He won't rest if you do anything to hurt me or the girl. So you might as well recognize that you're not going to get away with this. Leave us alone, and we won't report you for trespassing on our property."

"Ha!" one of them laughed bitterly. "Trespassing is the least of your problems, old man.

Our demands are nonnegotiable. Give us the girl, and we'll be on our way."

"What are you going to do? Kill her? If you try to take her, you'll have to go through me first."

What was his dad doing? He wasn't supposed to threaten the intruders in any way. Steven squinted down at the men. They seemed to be shrugging their shoulders.

"Look, we prefer to keep things clean and simple. Too many bodies are messy and hard to deal with." Bickler shrugged. "But hey, it's your call. If you want to go down fighting, we can do it that way as well. I've never been afraid to pull the trigger."

There! That was what they needed! But would that vague threat hold up in court? It didn't matter at that point since the man had threatened to kidnap Polly. This was the moment when Seb and his deputies were supposed to reveal themselves and grab the criminals. But no one seemed to be moving. His father was staring at the intruders, his hand still across her shoulders as he protected the girl.

"Well, I guess we're going to have to do this the hard way then," the man with the gray beard said as he lifted up his gun and pointed it at Scott. The other two did the same.

Steven raised his head, uncaring if he drew attention to himself up in the loft. Where was Seb? Why weren't they stopping this?

There! Two deputies seemed to have materialized behind the intruders. But they were too late.

Bang! Bang! Bang!

"No!" Steven couldn't stop the scream that escaped from his lips as he watched two bodies crumple to the ground.

SIXTEEN

"No!" Steven screamed again as he leaped from the hayloft. He needed to do something, since obviously the plan had gone dreadfully wrong.

Too late, he realized the folly of his action. It was a twenty-foot drop from the loft to the floor. Sure, he and Seb had made the jump when they were kids. But it had hurt even then, with a pile of hay to lessen the impact.

His body crashed into another person, but it wasn't one of the intruders, unfortunately. It was Seb, who seemed to have appeared from nowhere, wrapping his arms around Steven and staggering backward as he absorbed the impact of the fall.

"What are you trying to do? Get all of us killed?" Seb's anger was palpable.

"Me?" Steven pulled away from his twin. "What about you? You let them shoot Dad!"

Seb choked out a scoffing snort. "I used to think you'd make a good cop because of that staggering courage of yours. But I forgot about your mile-wide reckless streak. Look around you, brother. Everything worked out just like we planned."

Steven turned to survey the scene. His dad was standing upright, grinning as he unbuckled the Kevlar vest from beneath his flannel shirt. The diminutive female deputy who had spent the last twenty minutes kneeling on the ground, with the bottom of her legs covered with hay, had also shed her long, brightly colored raincoat to reveal her own bulletproof vest. All three of the intruders were now in handcuffs and surrounded by a half-dozen deputies. A feeling of chagrin crept up Steven's spine as his cheeks burned with embarrassment.

"Right. Well, thanks for catching me." He paused, then said, "I guess we did it then."

"We?" His brother's voice held just a bit of mockery. "You nearly blew the whole thing. Good thing Dad was able to follow the plan. Hopefully, once we examine their phones, we'll have enough evidence to convict them of attempted kidnapping and murder."

"So it's over?" Steven still couldn't quite believe what had just happened.

"Well, for me, it's just the beginning. I'm going to have to write a whole bunch of reports, explaining how I let a fugitive hide in my jurisdiction. Probably the FBI will want to take this one over. But, yeah, I get your meaning. It's over."

Steven closed his eyes and sighed, relief pouring through body. *Thank You, God.* He sidled over to his father. "You okay, Dad?"

"I might be a bit sore for a few days, but I'm fine." Scott was still brushing hay off his shirt, but a smirk was playing on his lips. "Nice to know that you've got my back although I'm still not quite certain what you thought you were doing when you catapulted off the loft."

"Right. Well, I figured I'd come up with a plan by the time I landed. I usually do."

"True enough," Scott agreed.

"I just radioed the sniper," Seb interrupted. "Etta and Lynn are still on the patio. We'll head up there and take Lynn in. Who knows, we might even be able to get her to turn on her son. Wouldn't that be the cherry on the top of the cake? Connecting the Texas attorney general to a kidnapping plot instigated at his mother's behest."

Steven shook his head. Trust his brother to be thinking about the case.

He quickly stepped beside his brother and another deputy as they started walking toward the house.

"Now, don't pull another stunt like you did in the barn," Seb said.

Steven nodded. It was a fair warning. Still, with her network of support gone, he didn't see Lynn putting up too much of a fight. And the two armed deputies who, along with the sniper, had been watching the house would be on hand just in case.

As they crested the hill, his parents' house came into view. He couldn't see Etta, but once again he felt a pounding in his chest.

It took only two minutes for them to cover the remaining distance. Steven felt an immediate urge to run over to Etta and pull her into his arms. But Seb placed a warning hand on his shoulder. "Let it play out according to the plan."

Steven grunted his assent as they continued their stealthy approach, waiting until they were less than five feet away from the women.

"Lynn Weber," Seb stated in a calm voice. "You are under arrest for your role in the attempted kidnapping of Polly Sanderson. You have the right to remain silent. You have the right to an attorney—"

Seb's words were cut short as Lynn seemed to crumple downward, only to lurch back upright a half a second later clutching a six-inch knife she'd clearly hidden under the leg of her pants.

With her free hand, she twisted an arm around Etta while holding the blade against her throat. "Take another step, and your girlfriend will die."

Steven stopped in his tracks. This was definitely not part of the plan. He glanced at Seb. The creases on his brother's forehead were not reassuring. He glanced upward, toward the roof of the shed. He could see the glint of the sniper's rifle, but with Lynn holding Etta in front of her, there was no way to make a clean shot.

"Don't move," Lynn screeched, her eyes flashing with rage. "I haven't survived for forty years to be taken down by a couple of no-account hillbillies from flyover country. I've disappeared once before, and I can do it again."

"Etta…" Steven began.

"It's okay, Steven," Etta insisted. "Polly is safe. That's the important thing. And you were the one who made that happen. I don't know what I would have done without you."

"Etta, no. This isn't over. I love you." Steven could hear his voice break. He couldn't let it end this way.

"You…love me?" Her eyes softened. "But I thought… Well, it doesn't matter. Because I love you, too." Tears were streaming down her face.

"Oh, shut up!" Lynn began to walk backward, the blade of her knife pressed against Etta's throat. "You—" She gestured toward Steven. "You can be our driver since this woman is so precious to you. Get the keys out of my purse. Stop stalling. Let's do this now." She let out a laugh tinged with hysteria.

"No, Steven. You stay here. Let me go alone," Etta said.

Steven walked over to the table and fished his hand inside Lynn's navy purse. Keys in hand, he headed toward the Mercedes parked thirty feet away.

"Don't try to follow us—" Lynn told Seb and the other deputies "—or she goes bye-bye." Lynn cackled. "Move it," she said, pushing Etta forward. They headed around the house and toward her car before Lynn shoved Etta into the back seat. Lynn climbed in next to her.

Steven slid into the front and started the

car. The sinking feeling that had been turning his stomach for the last several minutes
suddenly gave way. He knew what he had to
do. He just needed to wait until the moment
was right.

"Put on your seat belts," he said, snapping
his own quickly in place. He pressed down
on the accelerator and pulled out of the driveway. He glanced at the rearview mirror and
saw that Lynn had lowered the knife and was
fumbling for something in her purse.

This was it then. Up ahead, a gnarled oak
marked the turn-off to the main road. That
tree had always been there to welcome him
home, even when he was bruised and broken from the rodeo. His breath caught in his
throat as he yanked the wheel to the right and
pressed down hard on the accelerator.

The last thing he remembered was the
crunch of metal shattering against wood.

Etta bit back a scream.

The crash seemed to happen in slow motion—and fast forward—at the same time.
One second, she was sitting in the back
seat with Lynn beside her. The next, she
was pinned by the impact of an air bag
pressed against her chest. And yet, some-

how, she had known that Steven was planning something and that there was nothing she could do or say to stop him. From his hunched shoulders to his grim expression, he was going to save her, no matter the consequences. As the car veered toward the tree, she knew had done her part to forestall the inevitable. Latching her fingers around Lynn's wrist, she struggled to grasp the handle of the knife. For a woman in her seventies, Lynn was surprisingly strong. But righteous anger fueled Etta's determination. In the seconds before the SUV hit the tree, she had managed to knock the weapon to the floor.

But her success came seconds too late as the air bags inside the car deployed, and she felt the impact of the seat belt pulled taut against her chest. For several heartbeats, everything was calm, as if she had been enveloped by a large white cocoon. But then reality came charging back, with the sounds and scents of danger.

Sirens were blaring behind them, and the acrid smell of smoke assailed her nostrils.

She was having trouble thinking straight or functioning in a logical way. But one thing she knew for sure was that she needed to find Steven. As the driver, he had taken the brunt of the collision. She needed to reach him to make sure he was okay.

She unclicked her seat belt. The inside of the once large and comfortable vehicle suddenly felt dark and cramped. With a start, she realized that the car was bowed in the center, the passenger door bent inward on the twisted frame. She pulled against the door handle while kicking the inside panel with her feet.

It didn't open.

Summoning her last reserves of strength, she gave a hard thrust and the door gave way, a few inches at first, but then wide enough to allow her to escape.

Tumbling onto the ground, she was surprised to find all her limbs in working order. She had survived the crash unscathed. But what about Steven? She turned back toward the car, but strong arms reached out to stop her.

Scott.

"It's okay, Etta. I've got you. Don't worry."

That's when she realized she was crying. "I need to help Steven. Where is he? Is he okay?"

Scott shook his head. "They're working on getting him out now. Ambulances are already here, and the paramedics will do everything they can. They pulled Lynn from the back seat. She was knocked unconscious by the crash, so she's on her way to the hospital. Handcuffed to the gurney."

Etta gulped in a breath of air. She hadn't even thought about Lynn, only Steven. "I'm so sorry. This is all my fault."

"Shush." Scott led her away from the car. "How could that even be true? None of this is your doing. But let's get you checked out as well."

Etta allowed the paramedics to assess her vitals even though she knew she was fine. Scott looked at his phone and then sat beside her as they watched the firefighters working to open the door on the driver's side of the vehicle.

"Sandy just texted that she and Polly are going to stay with Tacy for a bit longer. They'll head for home once everything's okay."

"Thank God everyone else is okay. Scott?" Etta's throat felt like sandpaper. "Can we ask the Lord to save Steven?"

"Of course." He closed his eyes and began to pray. "Heavenly Lord, please give Steven strength. Be with him and with the brave men and women working to save his life. We know that You never fail us, even in times of trial. Please give us the courage and faith to trust in You. How great Thou art. Amen."

Etta looked at Scott. He didn't know—how could he?—that he had chosen the perfect words to sustain her through this trial. She reached over and squeezed his hand.

They both sat in silence, watching the activity around the Mercedes. Suddenly, there was an exclamation as one of the men shouted, "We got it open." The driver's side door was removed, and two paramedics climbed inside. Etta held her breath. Her insides felt wound tighter than a taut coil. The minutes felt like hours as they waited to see what would happen next.

Finally, Stephen's body was pulled out and laid on the waiting gurney. He was surrounded by paramedics, so she couldn't see much of what was going on. She and Scott stood up as Seb walked over to them, his face weary and tired. But there was a brightness in his eyes that was reassuring.

"He's unconscious, but his vitals look good. And he may have rebroken a few of his ribs. They're taking him to Mercy Hospital to see if he needs surgery. You two can ride with me."

Etta closed her eyes. Steven was okay. *Amen* silently echoed in her heart. Nothing else really mattered.

She climbed into the back seat of Seb's truck, glad for some time alone with her thoughts.

Then again, maybe those thoughts were too confusing to even contemplate. Steven had said that he loved her. And she loved him. But that had been true fifteen years ago, and things hadn't worked out. Who could say it wasn't even more complicated this time around? Switch out her role as her sister's guardian for her responsibilities to the child who had been left in her care. And while it was true that it wouldn't be long before Greg was released from prison, she was now even more determined to remain a part of their lives. Polly needed stability, and that meant more than occasional visits at Christmas and birthdays. It meant an aunt who lived nearby. And Steven's family was in South Dakota, which, as she well knew, was almost thirteen hundred miles away.

Etta sighed. Just a few minutes ago she had been basking in Steven's declaration of love. But already she was putting up roadblocks to any future entanglements.

Seb kept to the speed limit on the drive to the hospital, so it was thirty minutes before they pulled in front of the emergency-room entrance. But Etta wasn't going to complain. It had given her time to think about her relationship with Steven, though ultimately she had reached no resolution. She rolled her shoulders up and down, trying to ease the tension. How could they ever make things work?

"Just got a message from my dispatcher," Seb said. "Steven doesn't need surgery, but they want to keep him overnight. He's asking for you, so why don't you head up to see him while Dad and I park the car. He's in room 203. We'll join you in a bit."

"Thanks," Etta said, forcing a tight smile.

She passed through the automated doors and entered the lobby, where she filled out a form for a visitor badge. Steven's room was on the second floor, but as she counted the number plates along the corridor, the tighter the knot in her stomach seemed to clench. She stopped when she reached room 203. This was it. The moment of reckoning.

But as she stepped inside, all the worry and anxiety disappeared in a flash. There was Steven, lying in a bed. He had bandages across his face and his chest, but when he saw her, his face broke out into its familiar smile. He didn't say a word but held out his arms.

She didn't hesitate. She walked straight toward him, stopping short to press his fingers to her lips. But just that quickly, she released his hand, her wide smile transformed into an anxious frown.

"What did you think you were doing back there, running like a wild man into that tree? You could have died, and then what? Seriously, Steven. If I wasn't so grateful to see you, I'd probably stop talking to you for at least a couple of days."

"I wasn't really thinking of the ramifications. When I saw Lynn lower the knife for a moment, I knew that was my chance."

"Well, I'm thankful for that crazy move of yours, which probably saved my life."

"Ah, shucks, Etta, I don't want your thanks. You know that." His voice sounded thick with emotion.

She looked at him and shook her head. "Now why does this seem so familiar? Blood-pressure cuff. Hospital bed. Feisty patient with a sweet, crooked smile."

Steven started to chuckle before clutching at his side. "Don't make me laugh." He paused, a serious look on his face. "But you know, this isn't at all like before. Last time, I was stuck in the hospital for weeks. And I had to woo you as an invalid. This time, the doctor says I'll be out in a day, so you'll be up against the full force of my charm. But, do you wanna know the real difference?"

Etta nodded. The look in Stephen's eyes made her heart drum even faster in her chest.

"This time, I have no intention of letting you go."

Well. That settled that. If Steven wasn't giving up, then neither was she. It was simple really. She just needed to push aside all the obstacles and open her heart to love.

He drew her toward him and then paused with his lips a mere breath away from her. "Does trying again sound like something you'd be interested in?"

He didn't wait for an answer as he pulled her closer for a long, deep kiss.

EPILOGUE

Three months later

It was the perfect day for a ball game. Cloudless blue sky, and the temperature was cool enough by Texas standards. And the Rangers started the series with a winning record. Just barely, but Etta wasn't going to complain.

She and Steven had come to the ballpark on a date.

Her mind flashed back to those days after the showdown at the ranch. She hadn't known then—how could she have?—that a deep, abiding kind of happiness was just around the corner, that all she needed to do was reach for it and hold fast. Despite everything Steven had said that last day at the ranch, she had still half expected that once Belinda and her accomplices were arrested, she and Steven would part company, recognizing the impossibility of making things work. But that wasn't how it had ended, not by a long shot. Instead, there had been a kiss, and not just any kiss. It was a kiss that promised a solution to any and all dilemmas, and many good things to come.

But before all of that, there were countless details to be ironed out. The case against Greg was dismissed, but Polly was still not talking. And though Greg had arranged for her to visit a therapist, she was clearly having difficulties dealing with her mother's death. Etta had charges of her own to face in Texas. Even with Steven backing up her self-defense plea, there was still the issue of fleeing the scene, which, to her great relief, ended up being resolved with a suspended sentence and a judge's order that she perform one hundred hours of community service.

So given all that, it made sense for her and Steven to take things slow and easy. Their time on the run had set a high bar in terms of excitement, but not so much in romance. But gradually, all that had begun to change. She found a less demanding job at a hospital near Dallas, which allowed her to spend evenings and weekends with Polly. And, over time, her short bob had grown out, and after a couple visits to a good hairdresser, her hair was almost back to its natural color.

Of course, given all the travel requirements of a long-distance relationship, she had been asked more than once if her return to Texas was permanent. Her answer was always the same—time would tell, but she was committed to maintaining a close relationship with her niece.

And when Steven arrived in town for a visit with a couple of tickets to the Rangers game, it was hard not to think about what had happened the last time they had been at a game together. But she had managed to shake off any misgivings. After all, Steven knew how she felt about his public proposal since she complained about it at great length, and quite shrewishly, she might add.

The visiting pitcher was warming up when Steven appeared at the end of the row, clutching a box of popcorn and two bottles of water in his hands.

"Long line," he explained, sliding in next to her in his seat. "Glad I didn't miss the start of the game. Hope it's a good one." He reached over to squeeze her hand.

And it was, though maybe a bit too tense for her liking. The Rangers' shortstop ended up driving in the winning run during the last inning of the game, causing a good deal of rejoicing in the stands. As she and Steven joined the jubilant crowd flooding out of the stadium, he looped an arm around her waist to guide her toward the exit.

"How did it go with the interview you had with that reporter?" he asked.

"Okay, I guess." Etta had been surprised by how quickly the conversation had turned toward her reactions to the upcoming trial. But what could she say beyond the fact that she was glad that Belinda Caruso was being held accountable for her past and present crimes. There were so many questions waiting for answers, but it would be up to the DA to prove how much all the parties involved had known about the scope of Belinda's plan. With plausible deniability, her son, the attorney general, had remained above the fray, though he had decided to pause his campaign for reelection. Etta wasn't sure she believed his story that he was unaware of his mother's deception and her true identity, but so far Belinda had resisted throwing him under the bus in any way. As for the fate of the rest of her henchmen, there had been quite a few legal shenanigans on the part of their defense. It remained to be seen if they'd pay the price for their role in covering up the murder.

"Finally, there will be justice for Lilly," the reporter had said, snapping her notebook shut to signal the end of the interview. And Etta had nodded, though she doubted that it would be as simple as that. Her sister was never coming back. Greg would do his best as a single dad, but Polly would grow up without a mother. For all of them, nothing would ever be the same. But, with God's help and mercy, they'd learn to deal with their loss and find a way to keep Lilly's memory alive.

"Hey." Steven looked down into the box of popcorn he was still holding his hand. "There's not much left, but do you want the last bits before I toss it in the trash?"

She was about to say no when something sly in his smile made her change her mind. As she reached into the box for a last piece of popcorn, her fingers closed around a something on the bottom, something square and hard, which she grasped in her hand.

"What's this?" Her voice came out as a high-pitched squeak.

One look at Steven's crooked grin, and she had her answer. As she flipped opened the lid of the red velvet box to reveal a sparkling diamond ring, he dropped to bended knee. "Henrietta Louise Mitchell, I got it wrong the last time, and that's on me. But I never stopped loving you, and I am hoping now that you will do me the honor of agreeing to be my wife."

"Of course, I will. But wait…"

The smile slipped from his face. "What?"

"Don't you think we should figure out where we want to live before we make a permanent commitment?"

"I actually thought about that. How about nine months in Dallas and summers at the ranch? It's not a long-term solution by any means, but it will work until Polly is talking again and we have a chance to figure the rest of the stuff out."

"Okay," she said. Even she knew her voice sounded tentative.

"Listen, Etta. Things are never going to be perfect. Our future is in God's hands, and we need to trust that our love will be strong enough to make it all work."

Love filled her heart, and she knew that with him, it would all turn out okay. "You really are one very smart cowboy," she said as her eyes filled with tears.

Steven slipped the ring on her finger and then stood to pull her into a tight embrace. A small crowd outside the stadium stopped and stared, but she didn't care. She, Etta Mitchell, loved Steven Hunt, and this time, she was happy to share their moment with the world.

* * * * *

Dear Reader,

As I considered my characters' faith journeys, the words to the song "How Great Though Art" began playing in my head, and I decided to use the grandeur of its lyrics as my inspiration for Etta's and Steven's road to forgiveness and understanding.

As the story begins, Etta and Steven are both already Christians, but they have traveled very different paths to find the Lord. For Etta, raised as a nonbeliever, the words of the hymn represented a moment of great awakening to a new Christian life. Steven, meanwhile, was reared on Bible stories and learned to love Jesus at a young age. But given the challenges of fame, it took time before he became fully comfortable with that grace. The hymn is a personal favorite of mine, too, and it has featured in many meaningful events in my life. It always stops me in my tracks and makes me consider the glory and generosity of God.

Just recently, the song was played at my grandmother's funeral. Like my two main characters, I was able to find comfort in the words that we sang at her service. My grandmother was ninety-four and ready to leave this life and meet her Savior. It is so much harder when the end is violent and unexpected, as it was in the case of Etta's sister Lilly. And yet, we, as Christians, can take comfort in the consolation that death is not the end for us. God is great. His works are great. And His mercy is the greatest gift of all.

I hope you enjoyed Etta and Steven's story. Thank you for taking this journey with me!

Sincerely,
Jaycee Bullard